Y0-BDF-976

"I will be honored if you will consider my proposal . . .

. . . not simply because of the circumstances that have brought it about . . ." Here he paused, a flush reddening his face.

"I have already given my consent to your suit, and we have my aunt's and uncle's blessing," she said.

Duncan still seemed to hesitate. "I am, you know, twelve years your senior, a man not too much at ease in the world of society . . ." Again he paused.

"I am aware of the honor you do me, sir, for I am alone in the world."

He regarded her solemnly, then said quite humbly, "I, too, am alone. And have been for too long."

They walked a little farther along the flower-bordered pathway. "Then you will marry me?" he asked.

"Yes, Duncan." She spoke so softly he had to bend to hear her answer.

She looked past the low garden wall to the meadow beyond, where she had so often walked with Robert. From this day forward, she must put all thoughts of him out of her mind. Forever.

VALIANT BRIDE

BOOK ONE OF AN AMERICAN FAMILY SAGA

Jane Peart

Serenade/Saga
BOOKS
of the Zondervan Publishing House
Grand Rapids, Michigan

VALIANT BRIDE
Copyright © 1985 by Jane Peart
Serenade Saga is an imprint of
The Zondervan Publishing House
1415 Lake Drive, S.E.
Grand Rapids, Michigan 49506

ISBN 0-310-46782-9

All Scripture references, unless paraphrased, are from the King
James Version of the Bible.

Edited by Anne Severance
Designed by Kim Koning

Printed in the United States of America

85 86 87 88 89 90 / 10 9 8 7 6 5 4 3 2 1

Dedicated To
IRMA RUTH WALKER, my friend,
whose faith in me and this series contributed
greatly
to its creation

Part I

Boast not thyself of tomorrow; for thou knowest not what a day may bring forth.

Proverbs 27:1

CHAPTER 1

"WELL. WILLIAM. whatever shall we do *now* ?" demanded Elizabeth Barnwell of her portly husband.

But all Squire Barnwell seemed capable of doing at the moment was to stare into the empty fireplace of the parlor in their Williamsburg home, and to shake his head, a bewildered expression on his ruddy face.

While waiting for some answer from him, Betsy reread the note she held in her hands. Then, looking up at her husband again, she tapped it against her palm impatiently.

Betsy frowned, eying her husband's appearance, which was in sharp contrast to his usual meticulously groomed state. Today Squire Barnwell's powdered wig was askew and the buttons of his waistcoat had been fastened hastily, as if a five-year-old had been practicing. *And it is no wonder!* Betsy sighed. The shock they had just received would unsettle the most staid of men.

Indeed, both of them had been badly shaken by a totally unimaginable domestic crisis. Practically on the eve of her wedding, their eldest daughter had eloped with her French tutor, leaving only a scribbled note for them to find after she was safely away.

Who would have ever believed it of the girl? Even though Winnie was prone to flightiness at times, to behave in such an irresponsible manner was inexcusable!

Really! It was almost too much to bear. Betsy smoothed out the wrinkled scrap of paper clenched in her hands and read for the tenth time the hastily written explanation. Her eyes misted with tears of frustration and indignation more than grief. A mother with four marriageable daughters prepares herself all their lives for the bittersweet moment of parting on their wedding day; and Betsy had been particularly proud of the good match Winnie had made with Duncan Montrose, a wealthy planter.

"Well, 'pride goeth before a fall'," Betsy quoted. That foolish girl had allowed her infatuation with the suave foreigner to render her witless, and she had run off with him. By now they were probably in Yorktown, perhaps already aboard a ship sailing for England.

Betsy bristled, setting her ruffled cap atremble. Winnie had gone with not the slightest care for the havoc she left behind nor the wrecked plans for the wedding only two months hence, not to mention her jilted fiancé.

William glanced over at his wife. Never in the twenty years they had been married had he seen her so upset. He himself was at a loss as to what the next sensible step should be. The silence between them lengthened until it was suddenly broken by the sound of lightly running feet on the polished floor outside the closed parlor door, followed by a peal of merry laughter. Then there was a tap and the familiar voice of their orphaned ward, Noramary Marsh.

"May I come in?"

As if on signal Betsy's eyes met William's in a long,

measured look. No words were needed to convey the thought that was born in that instant. Noramary, William's step-niece whom they had taken into their home when she was twelve, was now an appealing seventeen—only a year younger than Winnie.

Quickly Betsy gave William an imperceptible nod, then, tucking Winnie's note into her apron pocket, she called, "Yes, dear, come in."

The door opened slightly and around its edge peered an enchanting rosy face. The coloring was perfection—the pink and porcelain complexion bestowed on country-reared English girls by a benevolent Creator. Masses of dark curls framed her forehead and fell in charming disarray about her shoulders. Her eyes were deep blue and darkly lashed; her smile, radiant. She was wearing a simple blue muslin dress and a wide-brimmed straw gardening hat that had slipped from her head and now hung around her neck, suspended by wide ribbons exactly the color of her eyes. She was holding a flat wicker basket filled with spring flowers.

Noramary was unaware of the charming picture she made, and of the silent appraisal her foster parents were making of her assets.

"I just wanted to show you the flowers I picked, auntie." Noramary smiled happily, holding the basket out so her aunt could see her choice. "The pinks will be perfect for the centerpiece tonight. Or do you like the daisies better?"

"Oh, yes, tonight—well, dear, they are lovely, but there is something—" Betsy paused, lowering her voice. "Come in, Noramary, and close the door, please. Your uncle and I must talk with you."

The Barnwells' eyes met again and this time there was no mistaking the message that passed between them. *Of course! Noramary!* Why had they not thought of her at once? Noramary would be the most suitable substitute for her cousin as Duncan Montrose's bride. Thus the family honor would be saved and disgrace averted, not to mention the sizable dowry already paid to the Montrose family by the Barnwell family, the latter not to be dismissed lightly, considering the Squire's recent financial reverses.

William Barnwell cleared his throat, turned toward the empty grate, and absent-mindedly extended his hands to a nonexistent fire. He had decided to let his wife handle this delicate matter. Although usually very direct, she could, when the occasion required, be very diplomatic. *An admirable woman*, he thought gratefully, *equal to any situation*.

Noramary stepped into the room, closing the parlor door quietly behind her, never imagining how this conversation was to change her life forever.

"Sit down, dear," Aunt Betsy said gently, gesturing toward one of the needlepoint-covered chairs. "A most distressing thing has happened," she began solemnly, "and we want to tell *you* before we tell the younger girls."

CHAPTER 2

LESS THAN AN HOUR LATER Noramary came out of the parlor into the hall. Stunned by what she had just heard, she felt slightly light-headed and leaned against the closed door for a moment to steady herself.

The shock of Winnie's elopement sometime during the night had been followed almost immediately by a second—the staggering request of her foster parents that she step into her errant cousin's place as the bride of Duncan Montrose!

"So you see, my dear, why we must ask this of you?" Aunt Betsy's voice rang in her ears.

Noramary closed her eyes, bringing back the scene which had just taken place. As her aunt had explained the dilemma Winnie's irresponsibility had caused and what must now be done, Noramary had sat very still, eyes downcast, hands folded in her lap, hearing but not fully absorbing her aunt's words. Now those same words burst upon her, strong and clear, exploding in her head.

"—marry Duncan Montrose!" *Marry Duncan Montrose!*

Distractedly Noramary set down the basket of flowers she had picked up and carried out into the hallway with her. Moving woodenly, she crossed over to the staircase and, clinging to the banister, mounted the steps with weighted limbs. She felt strangely burdened, frightened and confused. Suddenly all the joy, the lovely, comforting warmth she had found here in the Barnwells' home, was slipping away. Once again, in her short lifetime, she was experiencing that sense of aloneness—like a little boat adrift without its mooring.

When she reached the top of the stairs, she went swiftly down the hall, passing Winnie's bedroom as she did, wondering how her cousin had managed to slip out of the house in the middle of the night, with no one the wiser. Pausing at the door of the room she shared with her other cousin, she listened for sounds of Laura's moving about within and then opened the door cautiously. To her relief, she found it empty. Then she remembered that Laura had gone for a final fitting of the bridesmaid's gown she was to wear at Winnie's wedding.

Will she wear it now—at mine? Noramary drew a long breath. The enormity of what had been asked of her swept over her. To marry a man who had been betrothed to her cousin—a man she barely knew, practically a stranger!

But how could she refuse to do as they asked? When as a twelve-year-old child she had been sent from England to Virginia, the Barnwells had opened their home and hearts to her. Where there had been no place for her with her half-brother Simon, newly married to the haughty Lady Leatrice, they had welcomed her here. There was so much for which she could never repay them. To Noramary, her duty was clear.

Shakily Noramary sat down on the edge of one of the maple spool beds, trying to bring to mind a clear image of Duncan Montrose.

The first time she had ever seen him was a year ago at Christmas time on the night of the Barnwells' annual holiday Open House. Winnie, who had met him at another party earlier in the season, had boasted to Noramary of "the attractive Scotsman" whom she had invited to her home. Winnie was forever falling in love. None of the infatuations ever lasted for very long, so Noramary paid little attention to her cousin's enthusiastic description. Besides, she was much too preoccupied with thoughts of her own beau, Robert Stedd. That evening, however, she had gone into Winnie's room to borrow some ribbons for her hair, when suddenly Winnie had called her over to the window.

"Come quick, Noramary! Duncan Montrose has just arrived! You must see how handsome he is!"

Curious, Noramary had rushed to Winnie's side. Peering over her shoulder, she watched as a man dismounted from his horse. It was already dark and, with only the light streaming out from the downstairs windows and the meager illumination of the street lamps, she had only the impression of a tall, broad-shouldered figure moving with easy grace across the cobbled courtyard.

He had tossed his reins to the boy stationed outside to attend to the guests' horses, then stood for a minute, brushing the falling snow from his caped great-coat with his tricorne hat. Then almost as if aware he was being observed, he had lifted his head and looked directly up to where the two girls were peeking at him from behind the curtains. Startled to be caught so handily, both girls had jumped back, giggling.

Later, downstairs, Winnie had brought him over to be introduced to Noramary.

At close range, Duncan Montrose was taller than he had appeared from her vantage point at the bedroom window, was Noramary's first thought. Her second was that he was every bit as handsome as Winnie had claimed. His strong features were classically molded, with skin bearing the bronzed glow of a man much outdoors. Although elegantly attired for the occasion, he was not the least foppish. His fine blue broadcloth coat was superbly tailored. The pleated cravat and ruffled shirt of white linen boasted exquisite lace trim, and the crested buttons on his gray satin waistcoast were of silver.

But there was something else about Duncan Montrose that Noramary now remembered. Something Winnie had never mentioned. Something compelling—a directness, an inner confidence without affectation, a maturity that belied his years. His was a strong face, a magnificent face, full of character, she decided. And then there were his eyes—clear, gray, thickly and darkly fringed, strangely searching.

But does anyone recognize a moment of destiny in life? Noramary asked herself as she recalled that first meeting. They had exchanged the usual pleasantries and yet, now that she thought about it, she remembered there had been something unusual about that first encounter.

As he acknowledged their introduction and bent over her extended hand, his eyes had held hers intently for a few seconds. In that fraction of time, everything surrounding them—the laughter, the music, the guests—momentarily dimmed, and something infinitely important passed between them.

Recalling that long-ago evening, Noramary remembered something else she had almost forgotten. When Duncan's lips brushed her fingertips, her heart had lifted lightly. Duncan had held her hand a little longer than necessary, raising his eyes to linger on her face. Noramary had turned away quickly, glad to see Robert crossing the room to claim her for the next reel.

Robert! With a sudden clutch of panic, Noramary

realized that in all the confusion of the morning's events, she had completely forgotten Robert! It seemed unimaginable that her first thought was not of him!

A half-sob escaped Noramary's tight throat. Robert—whom she loved so dearly and who loved her, too. From a childhood friendship, their relationship had progressed into a romantic attachment special to both of them. And at Christmas, Robert had asked her to marry him. Of course, it was their secret. Robert still had to finish his studies at nearby William and Mary College, before entering medical practice with his guardian, Dr. Hugh Stedd.

Robert! He would have to be told of these startling new circumstances which would affect their future. Even now he was probably waiting for her at their meeting place. He was free now during these days of spring holiday, and during his visit at the Barnwells last evening, they had made plans for this afternoon.

Thinking of last evening, Noramary shook her head in remembered amazement. Winnie had seemed her usual self, not betraying by a single telltale look or word or action her own secret plans. And Monsieur, dropping by so casually, all respect and circumspect behavior toward the Barnwells, whom he was to place in the most awkward position imaginable. What a wily pair they had been! Noramary wondered if her pretty cousin had acted upon whim or impulse. It seemed unlike Winnie to plot such an escapade while in the midst of fittings for her trousseau and the flurry of pre-wedding festivities. The whole episode defied understanding.

But now Noramary was to pay the piper for the tune Winnie had danced to!

Slow, hot tears began rolling down Noramary's cheeks. How was she ever to tell Robert? How could she explain her obligation to the Barnwells? How to make him understand what she must do?

Although the families were longtime friends, neither suspected that Robert and Noramary had discussed anything so serious as marriage. Noramary had purposely delayed saying anything to Aunt Betsy and Uncle William because it was an unwritten law of Williamsburg society that the eldest daughter must be wed before the younger daughters followed suit.

Noramary's own plans must be deferred until Winnie was happily settled, though she had never doubted both families would give their blessing to the match. After Winnie's wedding to Duncan Montrose, Noramary and Robert had planned to announce their engagement. Now everything had changed.

Noramary could no longer restrain her tears as she thought how much Robert meant to her and how painful it would be give him up.

Almost from the first they had been drawn to each other by the parallel circumstances of their lives. Noramary and Robert were both orphans and, so, set apart. Unlike Noramary, who was penniless and without family or fortune, Robert had an assured future. The only relative of the prosperous physician, he had been adopted by Dr. Stedd and made his sole heir. Besides this, at age twenty-one, he would inherit the combined legacies of wealth, land, and property of his own parents.

Well aware of her own precarious position as a young woman without the dowry required to attract a suitable husband, Noramary was particularly grateful for Robert's devotion. This fact also assured her of the Barnwells' approval when the time came to declare their love and desire for marriage. But aside from all practical considerations, they had loved each other with a shining, incandescent affection that transcended the thought of dowries or property or inheritances.

She knew Robert loved her unconditionally. He teased her, made her laugh, plied her with compliments, set her at ease. Now she was being asked to relinquish the one person in the world who made her feel cherished and needed. Because of her childhood pain, the rejection she had felt at the hands of her imperious sister-in-law, there resided a deep insecurity beneath Noramary's tranquil manner. This feeling stemmed from the time she had been sent to live in a strange land, among strangers, though her sense of isolation had gradually diminished in the busy, cheerful Barnwell household. Instinctively, Noramary equated love with being lovable. She thought if she were helpful, well-behaved and sweet-tempered, she would win the love she yearned for. It was a kind of wistful longing to belong, beyond the dictates of her own faith and conscience, that drove her to be more obedient, more generous, more gracious than any of the other children and so earn a place for herself. Since the Barnwells had treated her with the same affection and tenderness they had for their own daughters, Noramary felt she could refuse them nothing—not even her life.

She must go now, Noramary told herself, wiping away the tears. Robert would be growing impatient. She must think how to break this terrible news to him. She stood, sighing deeply, knowing she could not put off any longer the painful task that lay ahead of her.

Unconsciously she ran her fingers through her hair, and, feeling the silky strands catch in the straw hat still hanging from its ribbons, she loosened the ties and took off the bonnet. Then she went over to the dressing table to brush her tangled curls.

Appalled by the reflected image in the mirror, she set about to repair the ravages of shock and tears. As she did so, her gaze fell upon the miniature of her mother, framed in silver. Noramary reached down and picked up the small portrait, a copy of the life-size painting hanging over the massive fireplace in the library of Noramary's ancestral home in Kent, England.

The artist had captured all the legendary Celtic charm of her—the graceful figure shown to advantage in the fitted green velvet jacket of her riding habit, the glowing complexion, intensely blue eyes, the masses of dark curls spilling out from under the small plumed hat. In the background was her prancing black horse upon whose curved neck she rested one graceful hand; in the other she held a riding crop. Every detail was expertly executed, even to the exact rendition of the Tara brooch worn on her shoulder, its emerald and diamonds sparkling in the late autumn sunlight.

She studied the painted face in the ivory oval, then looked searchingly into the mirror, and the words of her old nurse, Nanny Oates, came to her.

"You're the image of your sweet mother, darlin', and you'll be just like her when you're a young lady."

Her smooth brow creased in puzzlement, Noramary recalled that a variation of these words was given to her later as an explanation as to why her brother Simon was sending her to live with the Barnwells in Virginia. Leaving Monksmoor Priory forever? Crossing the vast ocean alone?

"It's because you're beautiful and *she's* jealous," Nanny Oates had told Noramary bitterly as she packed her little trunk for the journey.

The old memory stirred uneasily as she examined her own reflection. Had Noramary, as Nanny Oates predicted, grown up to look like her celebrated mother? Noramary frowned. Her face seemed quite ordinary to her, but in her naïveté, she did not realize that even a work of art viewed daily begins to appear commonplace.

Noramary had never known her mother, for Eleanora Marsh had died giving her birth. Instead, she had been reared in a house that mourned its young mistress, the second wife of a deeply grieving master. Nanny Oates had done her best and loved Noramary as dearly as she had loved Eleanora before her.

Simon, a half-brother and older by twelve years, had inherited everything at their father's death—the palatial manor house, the vast lands and properties. There had been no provision in the will for Noramary. It was simply assumed that, when the time came, Simon would arrange a dowry and a suitable marriage for his little half-sister.

No one had counted on Simon's marrying a woman who would bring such drastic changes in the heretofore rather careless life of the Marsh home and eventually send away the girl child whose promising beauty she feared.

Now Noramary had pieced together the truth and was learning that beauty can, indeed, be a curse—a cause of unhappiness in the life on whom it is bestowed.

"But why must I go?" the childish Noramary had demanded of Nanny.

The old woman's face contorted as she replied, "Because not many can stand the sight of beauty that's not their own. Ofttimes it brings out the worst in people—lust in men, envy in women." She had jerked her head meaningfully in the direction of the suite occupied by the Lady Leatrice Marsh.

"She's jealous, she is, my pet. She can't abide the thought that in a short time, you'll outshine her. Her's is the kind of beauty that fades quickly. Give her a few years of childbearing—and she must have at least three bairns, a boy among them—and her looks will go. *You* have the bones and bearin', the inner glow, that makes beauty real, makes it last!"

Thinking back to that long-ago day when all the arrangements had been completed for her departure for America, Noramary remembered when the reality had struck her full force. It was when she realized Nanny Oates would not be coming with her! She had flung herself into the old nurse's arms, sobbing.

Rocking her as she tried to comfort her beloved

charge, Nanny had murmured over and over, "It's God's will, dearie, God's will. 'Tisn't ours to question. We must accept it."

Now Noramary wondered, was this, too, God's will for her? Turning from the mirror, Noramary threw herself onto her knees beside the bed and buried her face in her hands as she hugged the miniature to her breast.

"Oh, why must it be like this! Dear Lord, help me understand!" she cried.

Then Noramary recalled what she had so often seen Nanny Oates do in times of stress, and she raised her head and glanced at the small Bible the old nurse had packed into her belongings to bring with her to Virginia. She picked it up and turned the pages slowly until she came to a passage she had heard Nanny pray many times:

" 'Thy Word is a lamp unto my feet, a light unto my path.' Dear Lord, give me the guidance I need this day."

Opening the Bible at random, she slid her finger down the page, her eyes following it to the fifth verse of the first chapter of Joshua: "I will not leave thee nor forsake thee; take courage and be strong. . . . Take courage then and be very *valiant*. Obey my laws and do not depart from them." Noramary thought quickly of the commandment, "Honor thy father and thy mother." Surely Aunt Betsy and Uncle William had been like parents to her. She read on: "Fear not and do not be dismayed because the Lord thy God will be with thee in all things whatsoever thou shalt go to."

Noramary closed the Book. Certainly those instructions were clear enough. She straightened her slender shoulders. Now all that was left was to tell Robert.

CHAPTER 3

NORAMARY COULD SEE ROBERT WAITING FOR HER as she hurried along the path toward the meadow. He was leaning against the gnarled old oak tree which, when they were younger, they had used as a hiding place for secret messages. Sometimes, even recently, Noramary had found a note from Robert hidden in one of the knotholes there.

Something like a hard hand squeezing her heart wrenched her at the thought that there could no longer be such notes, no longer the sweet camaraderie they had known through the years. Everything had changed—just since early morning!

Suddenly Noramary halted, chilled by the realization how, without warning, the wanton act of two others had utterly and irrevocably altered her life— and Robert's. Her eyes stung with involuntary tears. What would Robert say when she told him about Winnie? He had always thought her a silly, empty-headed flirt. Now that her action would affect him so drastically, what would he think?

Noramary stood there a moment longer, uncon-

23

sciously delaying the telling, and watched Robert stoop, gather up a handful of pebbles and send them skipping over the smooth surface of the pond at the end of the meadow.

How handsome he is, she thought, how free and graceful the movements of his lithe body as he tossed the stones, the full sleeves of his white linen shirt billowing, the sun glistening in tawny lights on his brown hair.

Noramary's heart felt sore and heavy within her. How could she give Robert up to marry a stranger? Robert, who knew her better than anyone else, who loved her with all her faults, who made her happier than she had ever been!

Knowing Robert, his enthusiastic, impulsive, intense nature, Noramary dreaded his reaction when she tried to explain the new circumstances that would change their future plans. His own situation with his uncle was entirely different from her own with the Barnwells. Would he understand her sense of obligation, her conviction that it was her duty to fulfill their request? All she could do was try to make him see what to her was a clear and certain path.

As she stood there uncertainly, Robert, spinning around to fling another pebble, saw her and waved both arms in greeting. He tossed the pebble, then started running to meet her.

"Noramary! What took you so long? I've been waiting for ages!" he demanded, the twinkling brown eyes belying the stern tone of his voice.

"My aunt and uncle . . ." she began hesitantly. "They wanted to talk to me. . . ."

"Well, no matter, now that you're here at last!"

He caught both her hands in his and smiled down at her, his square, white teeth contrasting with the glowing tan of his lean face, his dark brown eyes shining with happiness. His arm went around her waist. At his touch a familiar tingle, swift as quicksil-

24

ver, coursed through Noramary. She dared not look up at the tall boy who led her over to the shade underneath the sprawling limbs of the old oak. He knew her too well. She needed still more time to gather the courage to tell him what must be told.

There had never been anyone like Robert. Up to now all their times together had been happy. From childish play and games, they had grown to enjoy so many of the same things, shared so much—the love of music and dancing, poetry and plays. They had laughingly called themselves "kindred spirits." They had laughed much together, Noramary thought wistfully. Robert had always been able to make her laugh even when she was a little melancholy.

"Let's sit down here for a minute," Robert suggested.

He spread his jacket on the grassy bank for Noramary to sit upon, then scooped up a handful of pebbles and tossed them one by one into the water. The two were quiet as the circles spread wider and wider. Noramary, poignantly aware of Robert's nearness and of the dread message she must deliver, grew ever more tense. Her world—their world—had fallen apart and she didn't know how to begin to tell him.

When Robert put his arm around her shoulder, took her chin in his other hand and gently tilted it upward to kiss her, she drew back.

"What is it?" he asked, the hurt showing in his voice at her unexpected movement.

She swallowed over the rising lump in her throat. "Oh, Robert," she began, her distress making it difficult to go on. "Something has happened at home, something that affects you and me . . . *us*. My aunt and uncle have asked something of me that I have no right to refuse, and . . ." She stumbled awkwardly through the difficult recital while he stared at her in growing disbelief.

25

Even though Noramary had anticipated his dismay, she had not expected him to react so violently. When her stammering explanation trailed off with a plea for his understanding, Robert jumped to his feet.

"No! I can't understand! Noramary, you love me, I know you do. How can you think of marrying another man? You must wait for me, darling. Another year and then I shall be of age. I'll have my inheritance—a house in Williamsburg and property besides. I'll be a physician, an honorable profession. We'll have a place in society. You will have everything I can give you. What more could the Barnwells want for you? Of course, Montrose is a wealthy planter, I know that, but they have three other daughters. Why could not one of them take their sister's place as his bride? Why you? Blast Winnie and her fancy French tutor . . . what right has she or anyone else to rob us of our happiness?"

Noramary shook her head sadly. "Robert, dear, listen . . . please listen. I've given my promise. I can't do anything else. No matter how *we* feel, my darling. I *do* love you, I shall always love you. . . . But, Robert, they gave me a home when I had no home. They were my family when my own family turned me away . . . they have treated me as their own daughter. . . . I can do no less than give them the same obedience and love I would give my own parents."

"Respect, gratitude, obedience—to a point! I can understand *that*! What I cannot understand is blind obedience—giving yourself as the sacrificial lamb! Robert declared furiously.

With that, he turned to Noramary, reached down and grasped her wrists and pulled her to her feet. His face was very close to hers, so close that his eyes seemed almost black, the pupils dilated with anger. His voice was harsh and bitter.

"And is *our* happiness to be sacrificed then?" He grabbed her shoulders. "Doesn't that mean anything?

Noramary, I love you! You can't do this to *us!* I won't let you!'' he said with desperate intensity.

Then he crushed her against him, his arms holding her fiercely, and kissed her with a passionate urgency neither had dared reckon in themselves before.

As he held her and kissed her, she felt for the first time the fire flaming up in them both, that promise of a rapture that would blind them to anything else. It had always been there, she knew. Perhaps both sensed it; yet, knowing instinctively that it was for later, they had been willing to await its fulfillment.

Now, suddenly, there would be no tomorrow for them, no future, only this day, this moment.

In spite of her brave words, all of Noramary's resolve melted as their kisses lengthened, intensified. It was with immense effort that she finally broke away, breathless and shaken. "Oh, Robert, we can't—don't make it harder for me. . . .'' With a broken sob, she turned from him quickly, and, lifting her skirts, she started running back toward the house, a slim, graceful figure, fleeing like some woodland creature—from danger.

On and on she ran, stumbling at times on the hem of her gown, sobbing helplessly, the sharp pain in her side matching the one in her heart.

Behind her, she could hear Robert's pleading voice calling her name. "Noramary, wait! Noramary!''

But Noramary never stopped until she reached the garden gate—and never turned back.

CHAPTER 4

A CURIOUS PALL SEEMED TO DESCEND upon the usually cheerful Barnwell household in the days immediately following Winnie's elopement. Even the younger girls, Sally and Susann, seemed strangely subdued in the wake of their older sister's rash action. Laura, on the other hand, reacted with rare excitement at the unexpected event that had plunged her parents into such a dismal mood, and wanted to talk of it endlessly.

Noramary, usually Laura's willing confidante and indulgent listener, was quiet and uncommunicative. And in the face of Laura's protestations that the turn of fate casting Noramary as Duncan's bride was highly romantic, the older girl maintained her stoic silence.

Behind closed doors, there was constant discussion between the older Barnwells as to how to break the news of their daughter's betrayal of her promise to Duncan Montrose and how most tactfully to suggest to him the idea of Noramary as his substitute bride.

"The sooner done, the better!" declared Betsy emphatically.

It was Squire Barnwell's unhappy task to be the bearer of such tidings. So at the end of the week, armed with a miniature of Noramary to refresh Duncan's memory of Winnie's pretty cousin, William left Williamsburg for Montclair.

Even though Montclair was situated on the James River, a hard day's ride from Williamsburg and thus removed from the possibility of quickly circulated gossip, the Barnwells, nevertheless, wanted to be sure the news of their daughter's folly was delivered to the jilted suitor with as much dignity as the situation afforded. Thereby, it was fervently hoped, the news would be received with understanding and forgiveness by Duncan Montrose.

Although Squire Barnwell's pride made him reluctant to set out on such an undertaking, he agreed with his wife that no time should be lost. Too, he was anxious to make the trip before late spring rains might worsen the wretched country roads, in places little wider than a trail for a single horseman.

In spite of the unforeseen event of the elopement and the aftermath of despair they had felt briefly, both Barnwells were fairly optimistic of the outcome of the journey. Actually both Squire and Mistress Barnwell had secretly agreed Duncan would be getting a far better bargain with Noramary than with their own daughter. Not only was the younger girl beautiful, but a sweet-tempered, gentle girl with a delightful disposition, in contrast to Winnie who could be petulant and willful. Noramary was also gifted musically, accomplished in needlework, painting, dancing and spoke French fluently. Yes, Noramary would make an ideal wife for the wealthy planter. Truthfully, she was much better suited to the role than Winnie would have been, they mused.

Still, even with this hopeful outlook, William had a few nagging doubts as he left for Montclair. What if Duncan, insulted by Winnie's rude and thoughtless act, should refuse their offer? Worse still, what if he considered the dowry already paid simply a debt of honor as compensation from the Barnwells for their daughter's dereliction of duty? Given his recent business losses, that would be a disastrous turn of events, indeed!

"Drat that headstrong girl! And that despicable Frenchman! grumbled William as he jogged along the rutted road toward Montclair.

A much more cheerful William returned from the Montclair plantation. To his anxiously waiting wife he reported that Duncan, although greatly surprised by the news, had received William's apology with admirable restraint. It had been his sister, Janet Montrose McLeod, a "formidable Scotswoman," lately arrived from Scotland for the express purpose of helping her brother prepare his newly built home for his bride, who had evidenced the most indignation. She seemed to take it as a personal affront to the Montrose clan.

However, when William and Duncan had had an opportunity to discuss the situation in private, and Will had suggested that he might consider transferring his marriage offer to Noramary, Duncan had had a most favorable reaction. He told Will he had been very pleasantly impressed when he had met Noramary and recalled her as being "a young lady both comely and gracious."

But he insisted he would consider such an arrangement only if Noramary herself was willing to receive him as a suitor, and that a proper time of courtship should be maintained in which they could become better acquainted. Then, if mutually agreeable, a wedding could be planned.

"Montrose is a most estimable gentleman," William told Betsy in conclusion. "Any girl would be lucky to have such a husband."

Betsy was quick to relay this observation to

Noramary. She listened carefully to her aunt's recitation of all that had transpired between her uncle and Duncan Montrose. And, later, when Duncan sent a formal note asking permission to call on her, she replied affirmatively.

Betsy Barnwell breathed a mental sigh of relief. Everything was working out for the best. Noramary was being dutiful and amenable, and in the end she would be grateful. True, she had seemed unduly quiet, almost melancholy, but that was surely due to natural maidenly timidity, Betsy assured herself.

Still, there was something odd in the way Noramary had suddenly refused to see the Stedd boy. Betsy had felt sorry for him when she had sent him away, crestfallen. Strange, Betsy puzzled, the two of them had always seemed such good friends, always taking walks together, laughing merrily, finding pleasure in simple activities. Why, surely these children had not been seriously—romantically—involved with each other!

But how absurd, Betsy continued her thoughts. Robert still had his medical training to complete, and he was only a year or so older than Noramary. Both of them were so very young—they had been simply affectionate companions. Marriage could not have been considered so soon. She denied the very possibility, though she had to admit it had crossed her own mind.

If this unfortunate thing with Winnie had not happened, Robert Stedd would have been a fine prospect for Noramary. But it had, and that was that. Noramary was being sensible and obedient—and, in the end, she would thank her aunt and uncle for arranging such a prestigious marriage when she had no reason to expect anything half so fortuitous!

CHAPTER 5

THE NEXT FEW WEEKS brought spring in a blaze of beauty to Williamsburg, but for Noramary, moving through her own private grief, the world around her seemed gray and bleak. Hard as she tried to be cheerful, it was an effort to get through each day. At night, her pillow was often wet with the tears she had held back.

A letter from Winnie finally arrived. In it she begged her parent's forgiveness for the pain her elopement may have caused them and for any embarrassment resulting from her broken engagement. She went on to assure them of her happiness, health, and asked for their belated blessing. In closing, she sent love to her sisters, naming each, and including Noramary. As the letter was passed around to be read within the family, Noramary could not help the hardening of her own heart. Winnie's own excuses seemed so blithe, considering the havoc and heartbreak her action had left in its wake.

The more Noramary considered it, the stronger was her conclusion that Winnie had used her courtship with Duncan as a foil for her real romance with Philippe Jouquet. She knew her parents would never countenance her marriage to a man ten years her senior, one who had no money to offer except that which he earned. But it was so like Winnie, with her romantic, rebellious imagination to plunge headlong into such an attachment, the element of danger giving it even greater appeal.

Often in the past Noramary had had to pick up the pieces after one of Winnie's thoughtless deeds, but never before had there been one with such serious implications.

Now that Winnie was gone, Aunt Betsy's indefatigable energies were focused upon Noramary and helping her step into the role her daughter had so foolishly abdicated. Duncan Montrose, a man of wealth and power, was too important to lose as a son-in-law, and Betsy was determined that it should not happen. Therefore, on the day Duncan was to pay his first formal call to Noramary, Betsy fluttered about her anxiously.

Tense and pale, Noramary stood in front of the dressing table mirror, tying the drawstrings of her second starched petticoat around her tiny waist.

Noramary was well aware of her aunt's desire that everything should go well on this first visit and that Noramary should make a favorable impression on Duncan. She herself was apprehensive enough, and Betsy's fussing over her did nothing to assuage her fears. She tried not to show her irritation, for she sympathized with Betsy's understandable nervousness. The fact that this meeting was very important was emphasized by Betsy's insistence that Noramary should have a new dress for the occasion.

"You're much too thin, Noramary. I don't think you've been eating properly." Aunt Betsy frowned as she helped fasten Noramary into the bodice of the blue faille. "This dress fit perfectly when we tried it on ten days ago. Now it needs taking in!" she sighed.

Noramary studied her reflection in the mirror, trying to see herself through Duncan's eyes. If he particularly favored Winnie's type, he would be disappointed in her, she thought.

Winnie was petite, doll-like, with pert features and flaxen hair. In contrast, Noramary was tall for a girl, wand-slender, with masses of dark hair.

"Blue is certainly your color!" declared Betsy, standing back to admire the effect of the lighter blue overskirt embroidered with forget-me-nots. "Do you need help with your hair?" she asked.

"No, thank you, auntie," Noramary replied, taking up her brush.

"Then come downstairs when you're ready, dear. Duncan should be here in a few minutes. I remember him as being very punctual," Aunt Betsy said as she went out the bedroom door, closing it softly behind her.

Noramary took a deep breath. This meeting would be crucial. She knew how much her aunt and uncle were counting on it to go well. She closed her eyes for a moment and said a little prayer. When she opened them, she regarded herself critically in the mirror. She *was* pale and thin. She leaned forward and pinched both cheeks to bring some color into them, just as she heard the sound of hoofbeats outside on the cobblestone street. Duncan arriving! She would have to go downstairs now. Aunt Betsy would be disturbed if she kept him waiting.

At the top of the stairs, Noramary paused, hearing the murmur of voices coming from the parlor, recognizing her uncle's jovial one, Aunt Betsy's light patter and a third, deep and resonant, that must be Duncan's. She strained to hear what was being said.

"In answer to your question, ma'am, the house is nearly completed. I have incorporated some of my own ideas with the plans of the architect my father commissioned. I have some fine artisans among my own people, and they are hard at work on the carpentry and cabinet work. I hope you will see it for yourself when you come as guests to Montclair."

"From what William told us upon his return from his recent visit, it will be one of the most impressive of all the manor houses built along the James River," commented Aunt Betsy. "Is that not right, William? Is that not exactly what you said?"

"Indeed it is, my dear!" This from Squire Barnwell, emphatically. "I must say, Duncan, it is a magnificent place!"

Noramary knew they were discussing the house being built on the Montrose land, the home intended for Duncan's future bride, the mansion to which he had planned to bring Winnie!

Noramary moved quietly down the stairs, still listening as Duncan continued."

"It has been my preoccupation for the past two years, I must admit. That is the reason I haven't come to Williamsburg more often. I wanted to be sure the house was ready——" His voice broke off and there was an awkward silence. Everyone knew the unspoken ending of his sentence would have been, "—by June"—the planned date of his wedding to Winnifred Barnwell.

Graciously, Aunt Betsy shifted the subject to a more pleasant topic. "And I have always been curious as to the derivation of the name 'Montclair,' Duncan. Is it a family name?"

"A combination actually, Mrs. Barnwell," he replied. "The first half from the first half of our surname; the second, from my mother's Christian name. Many of the ideas for the house were hers; she made drawings from which our architect drew his plans. Of course, sadly, she didn't live to see them realized. As you know, she suffered delicate health and never moved to the plantation from our town house. In recent months I've been living on the property in the architect's model, a small cottage on the other side of the creek that runs through the land. Since my sister Janet arrived from Scotland, we have been using that part of the house that's finished while the rest is being completed. That way, she can oversee the workmen, arrange the furniture—" Again Duncan's voice trailed away significantly.

Just then Noramary stepped into the doorway and stood there hesitantly. Duncan saw her first, and Aunt Betsy, following his glance, nodded and smiled encouragingly. "Why, here's our Noramary now! Come in, my dear."

As Noramary entered the room, Duncan rose and she was again struck by his impressive height. She came forward and curtsied as he took a few steps toward her and bowed over her proffered hand.

Noramary, who before had only regarded Duncan with the natural curiosity given her cousin's intended, now saw the man from an entirely new perspective. He was impeccably dressed in a tan coat, immaculate white ruffled linen, yellow waistcoat. His russet hair was unpowdered, smoothly groomed, tied with a brown swallow-tailed grosgrain ribbon.

As she looked up at him, she again noticed the noble mold of his features, the steady gaze of clear, gray eyes.

She took a seat beside her aunt on the loveseat opposite Duncan, and the conversation began to flow once more. Noramary observed, with interest, that his manner was genuinely warm and unaffected.

"Montclair is not as isolated as it seemed in earlier days, for many Williamsburg families have built magnificent homes along the river convenient to load their tobacco on barges to take to market. My closest neighbors and good friends are the Camerons, whom you may know." There was a murmur of assent from the Barnwells. "Although the plantation social season is not quite as lively as in Williamsburg, there is much visiting back and forth and partying, a celebration for any and every occasion." Here Duncan laughed. "Like most Virginians we planters enjoy good times, and get-togethers are frequent. In winter, the roads do get rather difficult, but then our winters are short."

Although Duncan's conversation was directed to her aunt in answer to her question, Noramary got the feeling he was trying to reassure her that life with him at Montclair would not be a dreary exile.

Uncle William then asked Duncan about his crops and the conversation turned to a discussion of the agricultural and commercial aspects of the plantation. During this business talk, an area Noramary was vaguely aware was of great significance to her future and thus of interest to her uncle, she noticed Aunt Betsy casting glances in her direction as if trying to ascertain her reaction to the prospective suitor.

When Duncan took his leave, he asked if he might call again at the end of the week before returning to Montclair to oversee the spring planting. Aunt Betsy assured him he would be most welcome. As Duncan again bent over Noramary's hand in farewell, he said, "A pleasure to see you again, Miss Marsh. I shall look forward to our next meeting."

Thus began a series of well-chaperoned visits signifying a courtship between Duncan and Noramary. Of course, Aunt Betsy was always present on these occasions and often, to Noramary's acute discomfort, would insist her niece play the harpsichord for Duncan or would point out one of her watercolors or a piece of needlepoint Noramary had completed.

It was during one such episode that Noramary gained an insight into Duncan's nature that she might never have guessed.

At Aunt Betsy's insistence, Noramary had agreed to play a new piece she had just learned. Fearing that her memory might fail her, however, she was moving with some reluctance to the harpsichord when she caught Duncan's sympathetic glance and, at the same time, noticed a twinkle in his eye. It surprised and comforted her to know her prospective husband was a man of consideration and sensitivity, and an answering smile of amusement touched her lips.

Indeed, the more she was with Duncan and the better acquainted with him she became, the more resigned she became to the inevitable outcome of this arrangement. Beyond his courtly and gracious manner, was a man of intelligence and wit. She began to admire his forthright manner, and what she had once judged aloofness she now determined to be only an innate reserve. She liked his lack of superficial conversation, his disinterest in gossip. In fact, he had absolutely none of the affectations or airs of some of the young dandies so prevalent in Williamsburg social circles.

Besides these calls in the Barnwell parlor, Duncan had escorted Noramary and her aunt to a musicale and to a supper party hosted by mutual friends and, once, he had even purchased tickets for all the family to attend a play presented by a traveling theatrical troupe, much to the delight of the younger Barnwells.

During the first weeks of summer Duncan called often at the Barnwell house and, in time, Aunt Betsy discreetly withdrew into an adjoining room, leaving the door ajar and Noramary and Duncan to themselves. It was on one such afternoon that Noramary sensed Duncan was struggling to phrase the formal request for her hand. Though Noramary felt they both knew it was a foregone conclusion that she was expected to accept his proposal, she still felt a certain degree of reticence in the tall man she had come to regard with appreciation. Perhaps he had entertained second thoughts about the agreement. Well, she would give him the opportunity to back out if he so chose.

"It's such a lovely day, perhaps we should go out to the garden where it's cooler," she suggested.

Solemnly, his hands clasped behind his back, Duncan followed her out into the soft balmy air, fragrant with the scent of many flowers. As they strolled along the narrow, gravel paths between the flower beds, Duncan at last broached the subject on both their minds.

"Your aunt and uncle have told me that you would not consider it unthinkable—I mean, if I were to. . . ." Here Duncan paused and made a great show of studying some tulips as if they were a rare, exotic specimen. He suddenly seemed so vulnerable that Noramary felt sorry for this proud man who had been placed in such a position by her cousin.

"I am aware, sir, that you have been approached by my uncle and given permission by him to speak to me . . . of marriage."

"I would be honored if you would then consider my proposal . . . not simply because of the circumstances that have brought it about. . . ." Here he paused, a flush reddening his face.

"I have already given my consent to your suit, and we have their blessing," she said.

Duncan still seemed to hesitate.

"I am, you know, twelve years your senior, ma'am—a man not too much at ease in the world of society. . . ." Again he paused.

"I am aware of the honor you do me, sir, for I am alone in the world." Noramary made the statement simply, for she wanted Duncan to know that with his proposal of marriage, he was offering her position, a home and wealth, none of which she now possessed.

He looked at her solemnly, then said quite humbly, "I am alone, too. And have been for too long."

They walked a little farther along the flower-bordered path before Duncan spoke again.

"Then you will marry me?"

"Yes, Duncan." Her answer was so low that he had to bend near to hear it.

Noramary looked past the low garden wall to the meadow beyond, where she had so often walked with Robert. She closed her eyes for a moment. Now that she had promised to marry Duncan, from this day forward she must put all thoughts of Robert out of her mind. There must be no looking back, no regrets. If she made this free choice, she must try to forget what might have been and to accept her life as it was. She thought of the flood of letters from Robert, letters she had finally stopped opening, being unable to endure reading his anguished words, letters she dared not answer.

"Are you sure? I would not have you act against your will, Noramary." There was a thread of anxiety in Duncan's voice.

Sure? Her thoughts echoed his question. *But how can anyone be sure about anything in life?* She had thought hers and Robert's future was sure. Now, she couldn't be sure whether what she felt for Robert was true love or merely the yearning to belong to someone.

When she had timidly questioned Aunt Betsy as to whether her lack of romantic feeling for Duncan might be wrong, her aunt had replied briskly, "Of course not, my dear. If the truth be known, *most* marriages are actually amicable arrangements made for reasons of property or mutual benefit."

Was Aunt Betsy right? Or was there possibly something more? Noramary remembered poignantly that flaming moment in the meadow with Robert when they had kissed for the last time, and the world had stood still. The possibility of what they might have together had trembled between them. Then it was forever lost. Duty had robbed them of knowing the ecstasy that was now beyond their reach. Would pondering "what might have been" haunt Noramary for the rest of her life?

"Noramary?" Duncan's voice prompted her answer.

She blinked as if from the bright sunlight, then clasping her hands tightly together, she took a deep breath and turned back to Duncan. She looked into the face so earnestly waiting for her reply. How strong he seemed, how steadfast.

One could trust that face, believe the message in those eyes, Noramary was certain of it. Perhaps if she could not yet love him—at least not with that rush of fire and excitement she had felt for Robert Stedd— she could at least return that honest affection.

As Noramary met Duncan's eyes, she realized if she were to accept his proposal, follow the expectations of her aunt and uncle instead of the longing of her heart, it must be done with no mental reservations. It must be done with full knowledge that with her acceptance, she put away the past with all its promise, all its possibilities, and relinquish her dreams of romantic love.

Perhaps the future with Duncan Montrose would yield a richer, deeper experience than she had even known before. In any case, she had decided this marriage was God's will for her and, in obedience to Him and to her beloved aunt and uncle, she would do it.

Decisively Noramary placed her hand on Duncan's arm and said very softly, "Yes, Duncan, I would be proud to be your wife."

With those words Noramary was rewarded with a special look in Duncan's eyes. It came to her with sweet surprise that Duncan felt a warmth for her that had nothing whatever to do with his prearranged agreement with the Barnwells!

CHAPTER 6

THE WEDDING WAS SET FOR LATE SEPTEMBER after the tobacco crop at Montclair was harvested and Duncan was free to come to Williamsburg for a few of the prenuptial festivities.

Although Noramary had wished for a small wedding, the Barnwells were too well-known, too highly respected to avoid a large guest list. Too, Betsy was anxious to offset any unfavorable gossip that might still be circulating about Winnie's elopement by doing everything surrounding Noramary's marriage to Duncan with dignity and decorum.

Noramary seemed peculiarly indifferent in the midst of the swirling activity surrounding her, but if Betsy were aware of it, she chose to ignore it. If Noramary seemed quieter, paler than usual, more passive, Betsy chalked it up to the normal apprehensions of any bride, but nonetheless sent up a frantic prayer.

"Please, no last-minute problems. Just let me get her safely married—"

She suppressed any stirring of panic, reminding

herself that Noramary, for all her fragile appearance, was a strong, sensible girl, and her word, once given, could be counted on.

Inevitably, however, a crisis did arise, and at a moment when Betsy least expected it and was least prepared to cope.

The week before the wedding, Noramary seemed to have regained her composure. She had attended several parties, gone about her small household tasks with her usual sweet calm, then quite suddenly, the dam burst.

Two days before the wedding, a servant from Dr. Stedd's brought a letter to Noramary, which she had taken up to her room to read, away from her aunt's sharp eyes. Only a half-hour later, the seamstress arrived to make a last-minute fitting of the wedding gown. It was after the woman had left and Betsy was helping Noramary down from the stool on which she had been standing to have the hem measured that Noramary burst into tears. Still in her lovely gown, she sank down on the rug, the creamy satin skirt billowing out around her.

"Whatever is the matter, child?" gasped Betsy.

Noramary could not answer.

"Dear child, whatever is the matter? Are you ill? In heaven's name, tell me." Betsy got down on her plump knees beside Noramary, patting the girl's slim shoulder.

"Oh, auntie, I'm sorry! But it's just everything! This dress—"

"The dress? It's lovely, dear. Don't you like it? It's French satin, Belgian lace—"

"No, no, the dress is beautiful! I was just think-ing—everything is intended for someone else—hand-me-down wedding gown, hand-me-down bride, hand-me-down husband! Nothing really belongs to me, and I don't really belong to anyone!"

Noramary's face was buried in her hands and she

43

continued to cry, while Betsy stood by, watching helplessly.

Betsy knew she must attempt to stop the storm before it became a full-blown hurricane. If Noramary were having any second thoughts about the wedding—nay, even worse, the marriage . . . she, Betsy, would just have to do something and do it quick!

At the back of her mind was the letter that was so recently delivered—the letter from Robert Stedd. That's what had upset Noramary so. Well, she'd see about that! And Betsy set her chin determinedly.

Inwardly she strengthened her resolve to firmly support Noramary, to see that she kept her pledge to Duncan, fulfilled her promise. Noramary would be richly compensated for any sacrifice that her marriage to Duncan would require. She was, after all, becoming the mistress of a mansion, with servants and wealth, the wife of one of the most prominent men in this part of Virginia. There were certainly worse fates for most girls in her situation, a penniless orphan.

She patted Noramary's quivering shoulders comfortingly and spoke in a cheerful tone of voice. "Now, now, my dear. You're simply worn out with all the excitement. We'll just stop now and have a nice cup of tea, and you can rest and tell me what's bothering you."

Betsy rang the needlepoint bell-pull by the fireplace, and soon Essie, the housemaid, stuck her head in its muslin mobcap around the edge of the door.

"Bring us some tea, Essie, and be quick about it. Miss Noramary is feeling a bit faint."

She eased Noramary gently into one of the chairs and took a seat opposite her, peering with concern into Noramary's sad face. The girl did look peaked, she thought. Violet shadows under the wide eyes indicated sleeplessness, the droop of the sensitive mouth bespoke melancholy. Betsy frowned anxiously.

44

"Now, what is it, Noramary? You can tell me."

"It's about R-Robert," Noramary whispered.

Betsy's blood chilled. Oh, not at this late date! Surely Noramary was not planning to back out of the agreement!

"I want you to do something for me, Aunt Betsy," Noramary continued in a tremulous voice. "Something I cannot ask anyone else to do. Will you promise me, please?"

Oh dear! Betsy felt herself tense even as she impulsively responded. "Anything, child. You know all you need do is ask."

Immediately she wondered if she had spoken too quickly, rashly agreeing to something it might be unwise to accomplish.

Noramary rose and went over to the small applewood chest, touched the hidden spring that released the catch to the secret drawer at its base and brought out a packet of letters tied with a blue hair ribbon.

Noramary stood, holding them to her breast for a long moment, then hesitating a second longer, she opened a small wooden box on the top of the dresser, and brought out another envelope. Then she turned to face her aunt.

"These are all the letters Robert has ever written to me. A few years ago, maybe two, we began leaving them for each other in a hole in an old oak tree in the meadow. It was a kind of game at first. A secret hiding place that made it special." She paused, biting her lip. "I'm not sure when we first began to know we . . . loved each other."

Her eyes, bright with tears, regarded her aunt solemnly.

"Did you know Robert and I loved each other, Aunt Betsy?"

"Well, of course, dear," the plump woman nodded, her chin bobbing, "we *all* love Robert. He's always been like one of the family. Dr. Hugh has been our friend for years—"

45

"No, no, auntie!" Noramary shook her head, her dark silky hair falling about the pale oval of her face. "Robert and I loved each other differently. Maybe at first it was like brother and sister, but later . . . we wanted to marry, auntie. Of course, we were planning to wait until he finished college, until he came of age, received his inheritance and went into practice with Dr. Stedd. And until Winnie ran away . . ." she stopped short. Two tears rolled down her cheeks and she brushed them away with one hand and bravely went on. "But now, things are different. I've given my promise to Duncan and nothing can change that. Robert will have to get over this—as I'm trying to do."

With some effort Betsy got up from her knees and eased herself into a chair. Noramary came over, knelt beside her and put her head into her aunt's lap. "Oh, auntie, forgive me for causing you grief, but I must ask you to do me this one small favor. . . ." She handed the packet of letters to Betsy. "I want you to keep all Robert's letters for me. I tried to burn them, but I just couldn't . . . they mean too much to me . . . it would be like cutting out part of my life. . . . Oh, auntie, I really loved Robert so. I shall always love him!"

Betsy's generous heart contracted at the sob in Noramary's voice. Her instant reaction was to gather her niece to her bosom and say, "All right, Noramary, you don't have to go through with it. We'll call the wedding off . . . no matter that we'll be disgraced, possibly not able to hold up our heads ever again in Williamsburg society . . . never face Duncan Montrose. You can marry your Robert. Be happy, Noramary. Life is short . . . love, fleeting . . . try to be content with what you have. . . ."

But Betsy's innate practicality prevented the impulsive words from being uttered. Much as she loved Noramary, she knew the wedding to Duncan must take place. The family's reputation was at stake; with three other daughters to be married well, Noramary could not be allowed to jeopardize their chances. Who would risk betrothals into a family if two of its members broke their promises to a man of honor?

"You must promise me, auntie, that you will keep them safely, marked that they must be destroyed without being read after your death—or mine."

"Oh, Noramary . . ." Dismay crept into Betsy's voice.

"*Promise,*" Noramary insisted.

Betsy looked into the sad, lovely face of the girl looking at her with such pleading. It was such a beautiful face, a face Betsy had often felt eclipsed the ordinary prettiness of her own daughters. But its tragic expression now touched her sympathetic soul. If there were only some other way. . . . Then her common sense asserted itself once more. There *was* no other way. The marriage *must* take place as planned. She drew herself up and said firmly, "Of course, my dear, I promise."

There was a tap at the bedroom door and after Betsy's acknowledgment, Essie entered with a tray. Betsy poured Noramary a cup of the steaming fragrant beverage and handed it to her.

"Now, drink every drop, Noramary, then lie down and have a nice rest. Things will seem much better later," she soothed.

Betsy helped Noramary out of the "hand-me-down" wedding dress, thinking fleetingly that perhaps they should have had a completely new one made for Noramary, then led her over to the bed, fluffed the pillow under her head, drew the quilt over the still quivering shoulders, and murmured, "There, there, dear. Rest well, now."

At the door, she paused and looked back at the small figure in the tall, canopied bed. *Surely Noramary will be happy . . . if not happy, content,*

47

comfortable, provided for. . . . She'll have a house of her own, servants, a husband of good family, of means. . . . I could not wish more for one of my own blood daughters. And almost unconsciously, as an afterthought, *And may she forgive us . . . if she is not.*

CHAPTER 7

ON NORAMARY'S WEDDING DAY the sky was overcast with heavy clouds threatening rain.

When Aunt Betsy entered her niece's bedroom quite early to bring her a breakfast tray of tea and toast, she found Noramary clad only in her night-gown, a thin shawl around her shoulders, huddled forlornly on the window seat, looking out into the gray morning.

A tiny flare of alarm rose in Betsy at the sight of Noramary's woebegone figure, and the possibility of rain and no sunshine bode ill for a wedding day. A vague premonition of something unpleasant stirred within her, a feeling she had tried to banish all morning with busyness.

"Come away from there at once, Noramary!" Betsy said sharply. "You'll catch your death of cold. Bare feet, indeed! Where is your robe?"

She bustled about, setting down the tray, finding Noramary's slippers, her warm wrapper. She held it out for Noramary to slip into, then poured a cup of steaming tea.

"Now drink this, dear. Then you must start to get dressed. Remember the ceremony is earlier than we had planned, since Duncan wants to reach Montclair before nightfall. . . ." Her voice trailed off anxiously as she observed her niece.

The girl was chalk-white, and had to lift the teacup with both hands to bring it to her pale lips to drink. Her hands were shaking so that the cup rattled in its saucer when she set it back down. *Oh, dear Lord, don't let her have a fainting spell!* Betsy prayed. Unconsciously she groped in her skirt pocket for the small bottle of smelling salts she kept handy.

Any further pursuit of what might be troubling Noramary was silenced by the briefest tap at the door. Laura's head in curl-papers looked in. "Good morning, Noramary! Mama!" she sang out gaily. She danced in and bounced on the bed where Noramary was perched.

"Well, how is the happy bride?" asked Laura, her eyes sparkling with excitement. Not waiting for an answer, she turned to Betsy, declaring, "Oh, Mama, my dress is perfect! I absolutely adore it!"

"Very well, Laura, I'm glad you're pleased," said her mother with an air of dismissal. "Now run along and see that the other girls are up and dressing."

Laura sighed, but hopped off the bed. "You're lucky, Noramary," she called out in parting. "Your hair's naturally curly. My poor head is sore from sleeping in these!" She shook her paper-wrapped head with an expression of mock pain contradicted by her happy little pirouette.

After Laura had skipped out the door, Betsy turned again to Noramary.

"I'll go now. But I'll be back to help you with your headdress and veil." She turned to leave, but paused. "Are you sure you don't want to have your hair powdered. After all, it is the vogue. . . ."

Noramary shook her head. "I'd rather not, auntie.

There wouldn't be time to wash it out before we start on our journey."

"Yes, I suppose so. I wonder if it is a good idea to agree to an afternoon reception at the Camerons? It will give you such a later start for that long trip to Montclair. But they are such good friends of Duncan's and so prominent, it would have been unseemly to refuse such a generous gesture . . . I suppose."

The Cameron plantation bordered Montrose land on the James River and both families had pioneered what had once been wilderness territory. Their fathers had been close friends and the friendship was a close and loyal one into the second generation. The Camerons also kept a townhouse in Williamsburg where they stayed when James Cameron attended meetings of the House of Burgesses of which he was a member. It was a large, impressive pink brick house, where they were known to entertain lavishly. They had offered, rather insisted, on giving a festive party for the newlyweds after the wedding breakfast at the Barnwell home, to which only a limited number of friends had been invited. Jacqueline Cameron, Cameron's glamourous young second wife, a beautiful French woman, had tactfully pointed out to Betsy that the Montrose family had many friends who might be offended even if they understood they could not be accommodated in the Barnwells' smaller residence.

"We would consider it an honor," she had told Betsy when she called upon her a few weeks earlier to request that the Barnwells allow them to give the party specifically for their dear friend, Duncan and his "lovely bride." "Duncan is so dear to us, and we are happy he has made such an admirable choice in the beautiful Noramary."

She had leaned close and, in a confidential voice, had told Betsy, "We have often been concerned for him, so magnificent a man to live alone. Your niece will make him very happy, we are sure."

An hour later when Noramary descended the stairs, Uncle William, preening before the hall mirror, resplendent in purple velvet knee-length coat, lavender brocaded vest, white silk stockings, shiny silver-buckled shoes, looked up and emitted a long "Ah-h-h. My, my Noramary, my dear. You're a veritable picture!"

Noramary was touched by the soft look in his eyes, now somewhat brightened suspiciously. Uncle William had never been demonstrative, but his kindness really needed no articulation. Noramary could see it in his expression as he gazed at her fondly. She felt the beginning of tears, a terrible tightness in her throat. He was the only father she had ever known, and, for the first time, she realized he regarded her as a daughter.

The tender moment lasted only briefly, then Betsy bustled out from the parlor, magnificent in mauve taffeta, elegantly bewigged, and wearing her pearls. She was pushing the two little girls, Sally and Susann, ahead of her. At the sight of Noramary in her wedding finery, they all stopped, and the children rushed over to her.

"Oh, Noramary, how beautiful you are!" they exclaimed.

She leaned down to gather them up in hugs when Betsy's voice rang out in a warning. "Careful, girls, you'll crush Noramary's gown!"

"Oh, auntie, I don't mind crushes like these!" and she held each of them a second longer. Her younger cousins were especially dear to Noramary. They had been her charges upon her arrival in Virginia, when Sally was five and Susann only three. It had been one of her duties to take them to their dancing class, call for them at Miss Spencer's Dace School, and put them to bed at night when Betsy was receiving visitors or was otherwise occupied. She had read many a Bible story to them, played with them, taught them songs, corrected their sums. Perhaps their care had made her feel most a part of the Barnwell family Now she held them close, experiencing the first real pang of homesickness.

Susann wriggled out of her embrace, spinning around holding out her yellow silk skirt, then making a deep curtsy. "Look, Noramary! Ain't I elegant?"

"And look at *me*, Noramary!" chimed in Sally, turning so Noramary could admire her twin yellow dress. She tossed her head, setting her coppery-gold curls bobbing.

"You're both sights to behold!" Noramary declared, clapping her hands.

"Enough of this! We must start or we'll all be late, and Duncan will be wondering what's become of us!" Betsy said briskly. "We'll go on ahead, Noramary. You and William will follow in the other carriage. Where's Laura, and where's Noramary's bouquet?" she asked no one in particular.

Almost as she spoke, Laura appeared, lovely in peach taffeta, holding the bridal bouquet.

There were several minutes of confusion and chatter as the ladies entered their carriage and pulled away. Then Uncle William solemnly offered his arm to Noramary and they went outside where the handsome gilt-trimmed carriage, hired for the occasion, stood waiting. A misty wind was blowing and, bending their head against the wind, allowed the liveried coachman to assist them.

As she took her seat, Noramary arranged her voluminous skirts. Her headdress and veil required her to sit well forward, holding her head erect, but William sagged heavily into the luxuriously upholstered interior. He beamed at her encouragingly.

"Well, my dear, so we're on our way."

Noramary could think of no reply, so she merely smiled politely and looked out the small window at the gray morning, hearing the sound of the clopping hooves on the cobblestone street. "On our way," Uncle William had said. But in truth, it was only Noramary who was on her way—to marry a man who was still little more than a stranger, on her way to an unknown future.

Her hands were icy under the lace mitts, yet the palms were damply clammy as she gripped the holder of the starched ruffle surrounding the bouquet of white roses and mignonette. She stared without really seeing as they traveled down the familiar streets, passed the houses of friends, and at length turned into the courtyard of the mellow-brick church where she had worshiped ever since coming to Virginia.

The horses came to a halt with a jangle of harnesses, and Noramary felt the movement of the carriage as the coachman jumped down from his place and, a moment later, opened the door for them.

"So here we are, my dear." Uncle William's voice nudged her gently.

Noramary started and slowly came out of her numbed abstraction. She turned wide, frightened eyes on her uncle but he did not see the panic in them for he was already exiting the coach. He stood at the door, offering her his hand. Hesitating only a split-second, Noramary carefully stepped down.

For just a moment she rearranged the wide paniers of her gown, adjusting her headdress with her free hand as Uncle William fumbled with her tulle veil. It was then that Noramary became conscious of a movement in the grove of trees at the side of the church.

Instinctively she turned her head in time to see a figure, half obscured behind a flowering shrub, duck out of sight. It was so fleeting that she was not at first sure she had even seen anything. Then she knew! She had recognized the swift, graceful stride. *Robert!* Here? He had come to the wedding?

Noramary trembled, and a faint, giddy feeling

swept over her. She drew a ragged breath and turned toward the place she had seen the darting figure. But there was no one in sight.

By now the mist had turned into a fine rain, and she felt Uncle William's hand under her elbow urging her forward.

"Come, my dear, it's starting to rain. We don't want your lovely gown to be ruined. Come along then."

Like an automaton, Noramary put her hand through his arm and leaned on him to steady her as they walked toward the entrance of the church, past the shadowy clump of trees. Noramary's face, hidden by the gauzy veil, was tense, its sad expression unseen.

From the moment they entered the hushed vestibule, Noramary moved as in a trance. She felt detached, remote, removed from the crowd of well-wishers, yet keenly aware of everything about her.

As she moved slowly down the aisle toward the tall man standing at the altar, Noramary was strangely conscious of the rustle of her taffeta petticoats, the squeak of Uncle William's new leather shoes, the guests in the pews as they passed, the scent of flowers and candlewax.

Through a haze she saw the smiling faces of her cousins who had proceeded her and now turned at the other side of the altar to await her arrival. The little girls with their flower baskets; Laura, in a posture of unaccustomed dignity, ready to relieve Noramary of her bouquet after she reached the altar rail.

Above all, Noramary was aware of Duncan Montrose—looking distinguished and handsome in a nutmeg brown velvet coat, creamy vest, ruffled jabot. And when he turned toward her as they halted at the chancel rail, his eyes held a new expression, something she had failed to see there before. If she could have described it, Noramary felt it would have been— *worshipful?* No, that couldn't be, she thought, though she could not think of a suitable word, but there was no more time to ponder, for the minister began to speak.

She did not glance at Duncan again, although she was very conscious of him standing beside her as they took their places. Noramary never raised her eyes from the starched surplice the Reverend Mr. Hewlitt was wearing. She stared straight ahead as he began the ceremony. The words struck deeply into her uneasy conscience. Desperately she tried to forget that fleeting glimpse of the figure in the churchyard, to concentrate on the minister's words, to pray God to still her confusion, calm her errant heart.

"You are about to enter into an estate that is most sacred, and so should not be entered into rashly or ill-advisedly, or without the full acknowledgment of both its sacrifices and its blessings."

Everything grew hazy to Noramary—the white flowers and flickering flames of the tapers on the altar, the drone of the minister's voice. Then he came to that part of the ritual she had been most dreading and his voice took on a deeper resonance.

"If anyone knows of any reason why these two should not be joined in holy wedlock, let him now speak, or, as he will answer on the dreadful day of judgment . . . forever hold his peace."

I do, thought Noramary, horror-stricken, as a breathless sort of hush fell over the congregation following the Reverend Hewlitt's words. *I know why we should not marry, for I love someone else. . . . Dear God, is it a sin to marry someone you don't really love . . . for whatever reason?*

Noramary swayed slightly, her knees threatening to buckle under her. Immediately she felt Duncan steady her with his firm hand.

The moment after the minister had uttered this solemn question seemed to lengthen interminably. Noramary did not move or breathe. *What if Robert is here, in this sanctuary? What if he should come forward, speak, deny the truth of my vows?* Noramary's thoughts collided tumultuously as the agony of waiting stretched endlessly in the too-quiet church.

"Duncan Montrose, will you have this woman to be your lawful wedded wife—to love, honor, protect, cherish her . . ."

Duncan's answer rang out with strength and conviction. "I will."

Then the minister was speaking directly to Noramary. "Will you, Eleanor Mary Marsh, take this man for your lawful wedded husband . . . from this day forward . . ."

Her throat was dry, and she had to swallow before she could respond, "I will," her voice barely more than a whisper in contrast to Duncan's clear response to the same pledge.

"The ring, sir, if you please," he directed Duncan, then to Noramary, "Place your hand in Duncan's, Noramary. Now . . . sir, as you place the ring on your bride's finger, repeat after me—"

Duncan's voice came steady and sure. "With this ring I thee wed, and plight unto thee my troth, and with all my worldly goods do thee endow . . ."

"Bless this ring, O Lord," the Reverend Hewlitt was saying, "that she who shall wear it, keeping faith unchanged with her husband, may abide in peace and obedience and live in mutual respect and love."

The minister now concluded the service as he covered their clasped hands with his and intoned solemnly, "If you undertake to live the pledges you have taken today one for the other, and have made them with pure intentions, true love and right spirit, you may expect the greatest measure of earthly happiness allotted man in this vale of tears. The rest is in the hands of God."

CHAPTER 8

At the second crash of thunder the horses reared, whinnying in fear and the carriage swayed precariously. Inside, Noramary looked over at her new husband as she clung to the swinging handpull to keep from falling against him. His profile was sharply defined by the intermittent flashes of lightning that slashed the blackness of the night. In that brief bit of illumination she could see the stern, almost angry set of his features.

Noramary shrank back into the corner, shivering, and drew the velvet hooded cloak more closely about her. Duncan turned, aware of her movement.

"You're cold, aren't you?" It was more statement than question. He quickly removed his greatcoat and put it over her lap, tucking it around her feet. "I've very sorry about this, Noramary. We should have stayed at the Camerons as Jacqueline requested, but I was too anxious to reach Montclair. I wanted us to spend our first night together under our own roof. I apologize for my rashness."

Noramary sensed that Duncan was a man to whom

apologies and the admission of poor judgment did not come easily and murmured, "It's not your fault . . . the storm . . ."

"Yes, but I should have known these storms at this time of year can be treacherous. I blame myself," he said brusquely.

He had to get out of the carriage several times to help the footmen push the wheels through ruts where the rain had turned the road into a river of mud.

It had been raining steadily ever since their departure from Williamsburg late in the afternoon, and now the downpour had turned the rough country roads into rivers of mud. Duncan had been forced to leave the carriage several times already to help the footmen push the wheels through the thick, oozing stuff.

Noramary huddled miserably in her corner. The relentless swaying of the carriage had aggravated a nagging headache that had begun soon after they left Williamsburg. It had probably been brought on by fatigue and hunger, for she had slept poorly the night before, and had only picked at the sumptuous buffet hosted by the Camerons. After the toasting and the farewells, she had rushed to change into her traveling clothes because Duncan was adamant they get started on the long trip ahead.

Perhaps adding to her discomfort was the growing sensation of homesickness as each jolting mile carried her farther from everything dear and familiar. Noramary was transported back in time to another separation, another beginning when, as a lonely, frightened child, she had traveled alone to her new home in Virginia. She felt much the same now, she thought sadly, only this time there was an inexplicable sense of foreboding.

As stinging tears welled up in her eyes, Noramary tried to picture the warm, cozy parlor at the Barnwell home, where she had spent so many happy evenings, and a painful lump rose in her throat. When would she ever see them again?

She remembered when she had confessed to Aunt Betsy how unsure she felt about marrying Duncan. Even as her aunt had held her comfortingly, she had said, "You must realize, Noramary, that it is much wiser for our heads to rule our hearts, to accept things as they are. Life, dear child, is full of pain and partings. Love is one thing; life, another altogether. If one is fortunate," here she had paused, "you may live out your life with someone for whom you feel a passionate affection, but for most of us, life is simply doing one's duty." This advice left no doubt that for a girl with no dowry, no inheritance of her own, Noramary must take the course of duty.

With a sudden lurching of the carriage, they came to a standstill. There was some shouting from the coachman and the footman, but their words were not discernible in the howling of the wind.

Duncan swore under his breath. "What the deuce is it now!" he exclaimed as he opened the door and sprang out.

Noramary, her heart pounding, her whole body aching with weariness, leaned forward and tried to peer out into the driving rain. This journey was taking on a nightmarish quality. The carriage had come to an absolute halt. One side seemed to be slowly tipping as if the wheels were sinking into the mud. Terrified, she could only make out the three figures of the men moving awkwardly, could hear the muffled sound of their shouts. There was a strong tugging sensation, a sudden, shuddering lurch—then, no movement at all.

They must have unhitched the horses, she thought and, just then, the carriage door was jerked open and Duncan stood there, rain dripping from the corners of his tricorne, his clothing sodden and muddy.

"It seems that it is worse than I thought. I'm sorry my dear, but the creek is flooded just ahead and washed out the foot bridge we have to cross to continue onto Montclair. I'm afraid we are going to have to spend the night elsewhere."

"Not *here*!" exclaimed Noramary in dismay.

A slight smile twitched the corners of Duncan's mouth.

"No. The little cottage I told you about, the one I lived in before the big house was complete, is just this side of the creek. We won't be able to get the carriage moving tonight. The men will ride the horses to shelter, and I'll take you on mine. There's a small barn where we can stable them, with a loft above for the men. We can spend the night in the cottage. It's quite livable, I assure you." There was a trace of a smile on his lips as he added, "And as they say—any haven in a storm!"

Duncan reined his horse beside the open door of the carriage and spoke in a calm, even voice. "Just put your foot in my hand. He'll not move. I'm holding him steady. Now, don't be afraid," he directed her.

Noramary lifted her skirts and did as he had bade her, feeling his hand firmly on her waist. She was hardly seated in the saddle when he mounted behind her, fitting his feet expertly into the stirrups.

"I shall keep my arm around you so you will be secure and not lose your balance. Try to relax. My horse knows the way and will take us safely there."

Galloping through the rain-dark night could have been fraught with terror had not Duncan been such an expert horseman and held Noramary so securely. Just as they reached a latticed shelter, the rain sliced down in sheets. Leaning forward slightly, Noramary saw that they were in front of a small gabled house.

Duncan dismounted, then his hands encircled Noramary's waist and he lifted her down as easily as if she had been a child.

"All right?" he inquired solicitously.

"Of course." She nodded, but she was shivering and her teeth had begun to chatter, for the rain had penetrated her cloak and she was chilled.

"We'll be inside in a minute," said Duncan. Getting

out a ring of keys and finding one, he unlocked the door. "Come, I'll have a fire going in a minute."

He held the door open for her to pass before him and Noramary stepped inside. Then he followed her, shutting the door and bolting it against the fierce wind. She stood to one side as Duncan walked through the house, his boots echoing in the empty rooms. She heard the sound of cabinet doors being jerked open, drawers being pulled out, the sound of rummaging as Duncan searched for candles. Then, after a short pause, he reappeared, holding before him two tall candlesticks, shedding a pale, wavery light. He set them on the mantlepiece above a wide, stone fireplace.

While Duncan busied himself laying a fire with logs from a woodbox beside the hearth, and kindling and pine cones from a big basket, Noramary looked around curiously.

So this was the house Duncan had lived in alone for years before moving into the mansion she had yet to see. The walls were paneled and painted blue. The few pieces of furniture were gracefully made and finely crafted. There was a deep wing chair and footstool on one side of the fireplace, a gate-legged table and a ladder-back armchair. Patterned draperies were drawn across the windows.

"There," said Duncan, standing and brushing his hands. The flames had begun to leap and the dry wood crackled as the fir took hold. "The fire should be going well in another few minutes and soon this room should be cozy and warm." He turned to Noramary. "I'm going out to the barn now, see that the men rub down the horses give them oats, and bed down themselves. I shall be back as soon as I can. Will you be all right until then?"

He started to the door again, then stopped abruptly. "Are you hungry? I can find something for us to eat, I'm sure, but—"

"Please. Do whatever you have to do. I can wait until you return."

He hesitated a moment longer, as if unsure whether to leave her. "I'll hurry then." And he was gone.

A gust of cold wind blew in as Duncan went out and Noramary shuddered, not only from the sudden chill but from a kind of nervous reaction. Here she was, still miles from her destination, virtually alone with a man she hardly knew. Another wild thrust of wind flung the rain clattering against the windowpanes, and Noramary moved closer to the fireplace where the roaring flames now sizzled and sputtered.

Her wedding night! Noramary felt a wild urge to laugh. What bride had ever found herself in such bizarre circumstances! But her innate sense of the ridiculous was edged with apprehension. There was really nothing very funny about spending this night in an isolated cottage with a husband who was almost a stranger.

Noramary moved even closer to the fireplace. As she held out her hands to the fire's warmth, the light from its flames glinted on the gold band of her new wedding ring.

It felt heavy and unfamiliar on her slender finger. As she twisted it thoughtfully, she remembered a day last summer when Robert had fashioned a ring of buttercups and slipped it on the same finger with a smile. "Someday," he had promised, "this will be a band of gold uniting us forever!"

How little they had known in those carefree days of summer how soon their dreams would end. *Oh, Robert! Robert!* Noramary's heart cried. *I thought I would spend my wedding night with you! I imagined we two would explore the mysteries and sweet intimacies of marriage together! I never imagined marriage with a stranger!*

CHAPTER 9

THE SOUND OF THE LATCH LIFTING and the bolt shoved back made Noramary jump. She whirled around as the door was flung wide and, with a chilling blast of rain and wind, Duncan strode back into the room. She was instantly jolted back to reality.

Duncan was her husband now—not Robert. They had taken vows before God and man "for better or for worse until death" parted them. All thoughts of the past and Robert must be put behind her. She straightened her shoulders, wiped away the few tears, and turned to greet him.

As Nanny Oates had darkly predicted when Simon had sent her away at Leatrice's demand, "Every debt in life must be paid somehow, the cost of everything exacted, in this life or the next." Would Winnie someday have to pay for what she had done?

Noramary quickly prayed that her cousin was as happy as she had hoped to be. She would not wish anyone remorse. She had been brought up by Aunt Betsy to believe that whatever happened, you made the best of it.

Still, a girl's wedding night should be . . . Noramary bit her lip and clasped her suddenly clammy hands together tightly.

"Well, all is well out there!" Duncan said heartily. "Luckily, there's plenty of hay and the men had stashed some provisions of their own in their pockets," he laughed, "scavenged from the wedding feast by way of the kitchen maids, I'll wager."

He looked at her with concern. "Now, we must see about some food and something to drink for ourselves. You must be hungry as well as tired."

Noramary shrugged slightly. "If I had known where to find things, I could have—"

Duncan interrupted her. "Nonsense! I wanted you to stay close by the fire and warm yourself. I didn't expect you to do anything. Actually, I don't know what we'll find. I come here very rarely nowadays, sometimes only at midday if I happen to be riding this part of the plantation."

Duncan lighted another candle and took it with him into an adjoining room. When he came back, he was juggling a round loaf of bread, something wrapped in cheesecloth, a basket of small russet pears. He slid them handily onto the gate-leg table and pulled it over to where Noramary sat.

"It's a meager enough supper, I'm afraid. Certainly not the welcoming feast I'm sure my sister Janet had planned for our homecoming this evening!"

"Will she be worried, do you think?"

Duncan halted for a moment, cocking his head toward the sound of the storm raging without, then with a slight smile, shook his head. "On a night like this? Janet probably supposes I was wise enough not to have left Williamsburg! There she misplaced her confidence, to my chagrin!"

"Duncan, you are not responsible for the weather! Nor for the storm or the muddy roads or even the carriage wheels!" Noramary admonished, with a hint of teasing laughter in her voice.

He looked at her, frowning, then gave a short laugh.

"You're right! I have taken too much credit, haven't I?" A smile tugged at the corner of his mouth. Then a curious look flicked in his eyes as he gazed at her. "You know you're really quite remarkable. Most women would have been in a fine temper by now with all this!" He threw out both hands in a gesture of futility.

"But it's no one's fault," Noramary insisted. "It couldn't be helped. After all, only the Lord controls the weather."

"True," said Duncan solemnly. He paused and Noramary was surprised by a broad grin spreading over his serious features. "Actually, we've been praying for rain. The woods around here are like tinder and we've been worried about forest fires."

"Really?" Noramary exclaimed, putting her hand to her mouth in a spontaneous burst of laughter.

"That should teach me to be careful how I pray, eh?" Duncan joined in her laughter, and Noramary realized it was the first time she had heard the sound. It was a rich laugh, deep and hearty.

"That bit of shared mirth seemed to break the stiffness between them, and the tension she had felt so strongly in the forced intimacy of the long carriage ride from Williamsburg eased considerably. By the time he had got down pewter plates from the pine hutch cabinet, set them on the table, found woven napkins and pottery mugs, the atmosphere was decidedly more relaxed. Duncan had also found a jug of apple cider.

"Only about half full," he declared, holding it up and giving it a shake, "but it will quench our thirst and take the chill off, no doubt. Come, you must be famished. You hardly touched anything at Jacqueline's party," he said sternly.

Noramary was both embarrassed and oddly touched by the knowledge that he must have been watching her at the Camerons' reception.

She took her place opposite him at the little table and was surprised when he reached across it and took her small hand in his.

"Let us ask a blessing on this first meal we eat together as husband and wife," he suggested in a low, almost shy voice.

Noramary nodded, bowed her head, and closed her eyes as Duncan prayed reverently, "Good and gracious Father, we ask Thy blessing on this food we are about to partake at the beginning of our life together. And on that life, whose path is known only to Thee, we earnestly beseech Thy help and grace. We ask this in the name of Thy Son, Our Lord, Jesus. Amen."

"Amen," whispered Noramary.

When she opened her eyes, Duncan was gazing at her. Her cheeks, warmed by the fire, flushed a deeper rose. The hood of her cape had slipped back, its shimmering blue satin lining framing her face and her dark, rain-dampened hair that curled in fetching tendrils about her forehead. Her skin had a dewy freshness and her eyes—he drew in his breath unconsciously. Those eyes—deep, sparkling like sapphires! A man could drown in their depths, he thought, in a rising tide of emotion.

As if he knew he'd been caught staring, Duncan quickly picked up the knife and began cutting the loaf of crusty, rough-grained bread, mumbling as he did, "This is not at all as I'd planned your arrival at Montclair to be!"

Noramary looked at him curiously. In all their meetings Duncan had always seemed so sure, so confident. It was surprising to see him so annoyed over this unpredictable turn of events. It also surprised her a little that Duncan must have planned their homecoming carefully. She had been so preoccupied with her own thoughts that she had given little attention to what he must be thinking and feeling about their marriage, about bringing her to Montclair.

"How had you planned it?" Noramary asked shyly.

He unwrapped the large triangle of cheese from its cloth and started to shave wedges from it. "Well, to begin, I had hoped to reach Montclair a little before sunset when the view of the mountains is best. Then when we went inside," Duncan continued, "there'd be fires burning in all the fireplaces, shining on the paneling and floors—newly polished for your benefit, I might add." He looked up, smiling. "Incidentally, all the wood used in the construction of the house is our own timber—white oak—and the floors are heart of pine, rubbed to bring out their golden sheen."

Again Noramary was conscious of another facet of this man that had, heretofore, gone unobserved. Duncan was really quite articulate in contrast to the reserved, rather stilted conversations in Williamsburg. That he was describing Montclair with such pride and affection was equally enlightening. Every detail of the house was of great importance to him.

"And Janet would have a grand supper waiting, the table set with our mother's English china and crystal, which now, of course, belongs to you—as mistress of Montclair."

Mistress of Montclair—Noramary turned the title over thoughtfully in her mind. Noramary . . . *Montrose* now. The name still sounded strange to her, but one day she would grow accustomed to it, she supposed.

"Tell me, Duncan, why didn't your sister come to the wedding?"

Duncan took a long swallow of cider before he answered. "A number of reasons, actually, the first being that she is officially still in mourning—although Angus has been dead for nearly two years. The second, of course, was that she wanted to have everything in readiness for our homecoming." He paused significantly before adding, "And thirdly, and I'm inclined to believe this may have been the most important reason in her mind, is the fact that after marrying my late brother-in-law, Janet turned Calvinist, and my guess is she felt there might be more wine, music, and merrymaking at a Williamsburg wedding than her conscience would countenance."

"Well of course," she dimpled prettily, "Williamsburg citizens are known for their hospitality. But I can scarce believe that your sister would withhold her attendance from her brother's wedding, when even our Lord enjoyed such occasions."

"The difference, I'm afraid, between strict adherence to man-made rules and rituals, rather than to the loving spirit He intended. But never fear. Even though Montclair is a distance from other plantations, your coming will bring on a spate of entertaining! Everyone I know is anxious to honor my bride."

Which bride? Noramary thought dismally. She could not help wondering how Duncan's friends felt about the circumstances of his marriage. Winnie's running off practically on the eve of their wedding had to have been an embarrassment to him, and now he was bringing home her cousin as her substitute. Would they pity him, feel that the Barnwells had taken advantage of him?

Before Noramary could follow this line of thinking to its conclusion, Duncan said disparagingly. "What a wedding feast! Crumbly cheese, dry bread—slightly turned apple cider!" He sounded disgusted.

Without thinking how it might sound, Noramary quoted impulsively: " 'Better is a dry morsel with quietness, than a house full of feasting with strife.' "

"Aha! Proverbs 17:1. My lady knows her Scriptures," Duncan applauded.

"I had a very pious nanny," she explained.

"A *nanny* . . . in Virginia?" Duncan seemed puzzled.

"But that was in England, of course. I've only been in America since I was twelve. I was born and reared in Kent."

"I didn't realize. I just assumed you had always lived with the Barnwells."

Noramary shook her head. "I came to them after my brother Simon married." She hesitated, feeling there was no need to tell Duncan now about the circumstances under which she had been sent away from Monksmoor Priory. "My mother and Uncle William were step-brother and sister," she explained.

"Do you . . . miss England? Your home there?" Duncan persisted.

"Virginia is my home now," Noramary stated firmly, then, "Well, of course, sometimes I think of it. But it was a very long time ago and . . ."

"You have made the best of things," Duncan finished.

To her astonishment he put his large hand over hers where it cupped the tankard of cider.

"I hope you will come to feel Montclair is your home, Noramary, that you will come to love it as I do," he said softly.

"Tell me more about it," she urged, eager to change the subject for fear she might display some evidence of homesickness, more for Williamsburg and the Barnwell household, than for faraway Monksmoor Priory in Kentish England.

Duncan launched into a description of the things he had built into the house to accommodate a climate and weather unknown to the original English architect. Noramary listened with interest until, suddenly, mid-sentence, Duncan broke off.

"My word! I am talking a great deal!" he held up his tankard and asked quizzically. "Do you suppose this aging cider has loosened my tongue?"

Noramary laughed a light, rippling sound that delighted Duncan with its natural spontaneity. He laughed along with her and rising, said in the pompous manner of an orator, "Let us drink a toast! For, upon my honor, I have never before been known as a

70

brilliant dinner partner. Of course," he added sheepishly, "this is not what might be considered such an elegant dinner, either."

Noramary laughed again, delighted to discover Duncan's sense of humor. "I never dreamed you were such a thespian!" she teased.

"Madam, I am *many* things you never dreamed!" he retorted with a broad smile that transformed his usually serious demeanor.

Noramary looked at him in astonishment, realizing that what Duncan said was true. In these few hours—in this outrageous, unforeseen situation—she had learned more about this man than in all the weeks of their decorous courtship. Duncan was not just the dignified, rather aloof, courteous but cool suitor he had seemed, a man of conservative opinions, a prosperous planter. He was a man of many layers. A man who could laugh at himself, as well as at circumstances, a man of consideration and kindness, a man of faith and humor. He was complex, with myriad emotions and feeling underlying the reserved façade. He was, in fact, very much like herself.

Amid much merriment they ate the simple fare, and the shared meal became a feast as if the dry bread were a light, moist cake and the slightly turned cider the finest champagne. The unpredictable circumstances in which they found themselves, and what their family and friends would think if they knew about it, produced more mild hilarity.

Their initial stiffness with each other had long since disappeared and by the end of supper they were both surprised to discover the other to be a most amiable companion.

Duncan filled the black cast-iron kettle with water to boil for tea and hung it on the crane where its rising steam sizzled on the still crackling hearthfire.

"Have you had enough or too much of this poor supper?" inquired Duncan.

"Just enough, and I do feel better, thank you."

"You know, just now when you so aptly quoted from the book of Proverbs, another came to mind." He smiled. "I, too, was taught the Scriptures by my mother."

"And what might that have been?"

"Two came to mind, actually. First, Proverbs 15:10. Do you know it?"

Noramary's dark winged brows came together over her smooth forehead as she pondered. "Hmmm. Fifteen, ten, did you say?" And she quoted slowly, searching her memory, " 'Better a dinner of herbs where love . . .'" She stopped short, blushing.

Duncan finished it for her. ". . . a dinner of herbs where *love* is than a fatted calf with hatred."

His eyes were twinkling and Noramary smiled. Love was a word that had never been spoken between them until the wedding ceremony earlier that morning: "love, honor, cherish." So beautiful, but love had to be more than words, Noramary thought wistfully.

For a few minutes there was silence in the room. Only the sound of the wind and rain blowing against the sides of the cottage, clattering like pebbles on the roof and windows, disturbed the peaceful moment.

Duncan refilled their tankards with cider and began speaking again in a more serious tone of voice. "When I started planning my house—*our* house," he amended, "I wanted it to become one of the finest of the James River manors. Only the best materials would be used in its construction—elements from our land itself. I wanted to build a splendid house that would endure for years, that would stand for our family . . . and those who came after us." Again Duncan paused, his eyes holding Noramary in an unswerving gaze. "Our family has been greatly blessed in property and possessions. Our land was originally a King's Grant deeded to my father and his brother. Unfortunately, my uncle died before reaching his majority and his part came to my father and his sons." A shadow seemed to pass over Duncan's face as he continued. "But my older brother James died of fever when he was still a boy and so . . . I'm the only Montrose left, the last of the family. The land is now mine and . . ." He left the rest of the sentence incomplete, its implication clear.

As the only male surviving, the owner of vast properties and wealth, it was understandable that Duncan hoped for an heir to carry on the proud name of Montrose. It was important, therefore, really necessary, for him to marry, Noramary mused, if not the bride of his choice, then a substitute. She lowered her eyes, crumbling the piece of dry bread in her hand.

A sudden clap of thunder caused them both to start, and Duncan nearly toppled his tankard of cider with the involuntary movement of his hand. In the ensuing moment, they rose from the table and Duncan strode over to the door to bolt it securely against the rising wind.

The interruption seemed to break the amiable intimacy of their mealtime, and as Noramary moved to stand beside the fire, she sensed an awkwardness between them once again.

She began to feel intensely weary. It had been a long day filled with tension and excitement, as well as the unforeseen hazards encountered on their journey. She had had little sleep the night before, she recalled, spending a good part of it apprehensive about *this* night.

Her wedding night! Here?

Before her thoughts became more agitated, she heard Duncan moving around behind her, his boots sounding on the bare wooden flooring of the rooms beyond. Curious to see what he was doing, she turned about just in time to see him returning with an armload of quilts.

"There are no sheets or pillows in the bedrooms, and the mattresses have been removed, but I found these in the blanket box and I'll fix you a place on the settle in front of the fire. You should be fairly comfortable there. By morning the rain should have slacked enough for us to ford the creek and get to the house on horseback. Later, I'll get help to move the carriage out." Duncan spoke briskly as he shoved the wooden high-backed settle at an angle to the fireplace and proceeded to fold quilts upon it. "Maybe the water will have receded and we can use the bridge." He turned to her with a teasing smile. "But, as they say, 'we'll cross that bridge when we come to it, eh?'"

Noramary attempted a weak smile. She felt worn out, but relieved at the makeshift sleeping arrangements. She was almost too tired to think of anything but curling up before the fire and closing her heavy eyelids.

"Come try this. See if you can manage to sleep on it," urged Duncan.

She gathered up her skirts, let herself down to stretch out on the narrow bench. To her surprise, the quilts felt amazingly soft.

"How is that?" asked Duncan with concern.

"Fine," she murmured drowsily, her eyes already beginning to close.

"Then, I'll bank the fire a bit, and it should burn through the night."

Through her half-closed eyelids, Noramary saw the flames sending patterns of light dancing across the ceiling. Then the firelight was temporarily blocked by a tall figure standing over her. She felt a light touch as Duncan placed the back of his hand against her cheek and said very softly, "There is another Proverb, Noramary." His voice was very low. "The most important one, more important than land or property or possessions . . ."

"Which one?" she asked, her voice husky with sleep.

"Proverbs 19:14," he replied.

She mustered a small laugh. "Duncan, I can't think what that could be," and sighed sleepily.

"'Houses and riches are an inheritance from fathers, but a good wife is from the Lord.'" Duncan's words were the last she heard as she drifted off to sleep.

Before Duncan himself bedded down on the opposite side of the fireplace, he stood looking down at his sleeping bride. She was infinitely more beautiful than he had ever seen her—dark wavy hair tumbled about her flushed cheeks pillowed on small, dainty hands; her black lashes, shadowy crescents against her flawless skin.

Noramary, so gentle and sweet, so warm and laughing . . . Duncan felt a sensation so sharp, yet tender, that it was almost pain. Hope flared brightly within, and the conviction grew that in her he had found the thing for which he had been searching all his life—love. The marriage had been carefully considered and, while he thought he had based his decision on the most practical of reasons, he knew now he was wrong. By the most unforeseen, the strangest of circumstances, this lovely creature had become his wife. Now, all at once, she was the most important thing in his life.

How was it possible that he had entertained even a brief attraction to her cousin, because he knew without a doubt that he had fallen in love—madly, wildly, inexplicably with Noramary, his bride by default!

Thanks be to God! Duncan's heart pumped gratefully. He, who had always thought love was for poets, the writers of ballads and sonnets and romantic plays, a kind of madness that a practical man like himself would never experience. How wrong he had been and how thankful that he would not, after all, miss this glorious insanity!

Now looking at Noramary, he was overwhelmed with the passionate desire to possess her, but he must proceed carefully, gently, so as not to frighten her in any way. The time would come. In the meantime he must simply be patient and wait. . . .

A log broke apart in the fireplace, sending up spirals of sparks and scattering red embers. Duncan turned to tend the fire.

Outside, the elements raged on, but oblivious to both the storm and her new husband's adoring vigil, Noramary slept.

CHAPTER 10

FAINT GRAY LIGHT seeped between the edges of the curtains. Noramary stirred, sighed and opened her eyes. She felt stiff and cold, then startled awake, confused. She sat up and Duncan's cape slipped off her knees. Realization of where she was and what had happened came quickly. She saw Duncan's long figure stretched out on the high-backed wooden settle opposite.

As quietly as she could she got up, stretching her strained muscles and arching her back a little. The room had chilled, for the fire had smoldered into a few glowing red chunks of charred wood. She pulled the cape around her shoulders and crept over to one of the windows and peered out.

Although it had stopped raining, steady streams of water dripped from the overhanging eaves. As far as she could see, the cottage was surrounded by a deep wood. Its depth was somehow overwhelming. Noramary had heard this part of Virginia was practically wilderness, but until now that fact had not particularly frightened her. But on this dreary morning it somehow seemed threatening.

At Cameron Hall the afternoon before, she had not had the feeling of isolation she had now. In their luxurious drawing room, illuminated by dozens of candles in crystal chandeliers, its yellow damask draperies, white marble mantel, graceful furniture and French wallpaper, they could have been in any elegant Williamsburg home. Here, however, a feeling of loneliness and desolation assailed her, and Noramary shivered involuntarily.

"Good morning! I did not think to sleep this soundly. You are awake and up already, I see. No doubt it was the comfort of your accommodations last evening!" he said with a trace of humor.

Noramary felt a little self-conscious, newly aware as she was of their relationship and with the merriment with which they had accepted their predicament last night somewhat diminished in the cold light of day.

"We'll have a cup of tea, then I'll ride ahead and take a look at the creek, see if we can get across it," he told her. "I'll make up the fire before seeing how the men and horses have fared through the night."

With his back to her, he began placing fresh logs on the grate, stirring up the coals. Over his shoulder he said, "There's a bedroom at the end of the hall, a mirror, the necessities, if you care to freshen yourself."

Noramary gratefully followed his directions and found herself in a large bedroom. She surveyed it with interest, knowing Duncan had lived here during his bachelor years. It pleased her to see with what taste it was decorated. A huge high bed with carved pineapple posters, covered in a plain, tufted woven spread. A fine English desk with a slanted top, a shelf of books and two fiddle back armchairs on either side of the fireplace, bordered by colorful tiles.

Noramary did the best she could with her small

brush, to untangle the damage done to her hair by wind and rain and a night curled up on the settle. She wanted to be at least presentable when she met Duncan's sister when they arrived at Montclair.

Janet McLeod had agreed to stay on another few months after Duncan's engagement to Winnie ended with the prospect of a substitute bride coming to Montclair. Noramary was grateful that there would be someone knowledgeable to help her assume her new role as plantation mistress, for she knew very little about running a household, especially a house as big as Montclair with a number of servants to supervise.

She felt some timidity about meeting this lady whom she had heard Uncle Will describe as "formidable," whatever that meant, Noramary thought with an inner quaver.

Having done all that was possible to repair her appearance, Noramary rejoined Duncan in the front room.

He handed her a cup of steaming tea, strong and unsweetened, that made her eyes water as she swallowed it, but sent a comforting warmth all through her chilled body.

They stood facing each other by the now roaring fire and their eyes held each other in a kind of honest appraisal, an intimacy, evolved from enduring together an unexpected but surprisingly interesting adventure.

All at once, Duncan felt overcome with emotion and turned away to stare into the fire to ease his own consternation. The words he wanted to say stuck in his throat. He finished his tea and set down the cup. When he turned back Noramary was still looking at him, a little smile tugging the corners of her pretty mouth.

He moved toward her, took the teacup out of her hand and, placing it on the table, turned toward her, searching her face as if seeking some certain response.

At that very moment there was a loud, insistent knock at the door. Impatiently Duncan took a few quick steps and jerked it open. It was Josiah, his groom, standing on the porch. He whipped off his hat and bowed low. "Horse ready to ride, Master Duncan."

"Be with you in a minute," Duncan said crisply. He snatched up his cape and flung it over his shoulders.

"This shouldn't take long, my dear. I'll check the carriage to see if we can get it out of the rut. The sun's shining fairly strong now. Perhaps the mud has dried some."

With that he was gone, leaving Noramary both touched and bewildered by the little scene that had just taken place between them. She could not imagine what her future with Duncan would hold. He was, she could tell, a man of quickly changing moods. A man who would be hard to know, but possible to love.

By noon they had freed the carriage from its muddy rut and were back on the road. As he had gently deposited her in the carriage, not letting her feet touch the rain-soaked ground, he had said to her, his eyes shining in anticipation: "I'll see you at the house." It seemed he wanted to say something else, but changed his mind and just touched the brim of his tricorne in a little salute, sprang upon his horse and rode away.

The sun had come out full now, breaking through the clouds in a brilliant burst of light, turning the raindrops still clinging to leaf and shrub to sparkling diamonds.

Noramary leaned forward, looking from window to window, as the carriage jogged along the rough road.

The country through which they rode was spectacularly beautiful, if wild. Through the rows of dense pines, flashes of scarlet maples could be seen. Purple asters and flaming golden shrubbery flourished on either side. As they came into a clearing Noramary saw a ribbon of gleaming light that must be the river sparkling in the autumn sun.

After what seemed a long drive, Duncan rode back beside the carriage, ordered the driver to halt the horses, then opened the door and leaned in to tell Noramary that they were now at the edge of their property.

"This is the beginning of Montrose land," he said with evident pride, as if he wanted her to take special notice of the landscape from this point on. "It won't be too much longer. The house is just two miles from the gate."

"I'll ride on ahead," he said and with a wave was off again. "We'll soon be home!"

Home! That word had meant two places to Noramary in the short span of her lifetime. Now she was asked to call another strange place *home*, and she wondered if Montclair could ever mean to her what it obviously meant to Duncan. A fierce longing for a place of security, comfort, protection—a place where she truly belonged—swept over Noramary. Would she ever know such a place! Would Montclair fulfill that yearning in her?

She leaned her head against the carriage cushions and closed her eyes, struggling against the welling tears, a wave of nostalgia threatening to overwhelm her. A picture of her childhood home in Kent formed in her mind—as she had seen it the day she left.

Monksmoor Priory—piercing the sky with its pointed gables, the sun glinting on the diamond-paned windows, the rosy stone. The house had been in the Marsh family for generations, its first stone laid in the fourteenth century. There was a topiary garden and

81

terraced lawns and wide meadows stretching for miles. She had ridden her pony along the chalky cliffs down to rocky beach and then the sea. There had been a vast expanse of sky, and the ocean thrusting out as far as the eye could see. It had not closed in upon you like these dark woods, Noramary thought, opening her eyes again to find the carriage edged on both sides by a thick stand of pines.

Leaning forward again, she looked out the small carriage window to see Duncan riding ahead, and beyond him, a wide gate flanked by fieldstone posts. Noramary drew in her breath sharply. Soon she would arrive at Montclair, get her first glimpse of the great house of which she was now mistress.

Duncan should be with her now, she thought. Yet, when at last Montclair came into view, she was glad he was not, so keen was her disappointment!

The house stood on a knoll directly ahead as they approached by way of the winding road. It was austere to the point of severity, an unpretentious square building of new, raw brick, rising three stories, with a sloping slate roof and massive twin chimneys at either end. Peaked dormer windows marched across the top; six windows along the second row, shuttered with dark green louvers; and, on the first floor, long narrow rectangles with matching shutters. The grounds, except for the surrounding elm trees, were not yet landscaped—not a flowering bush nor any sign of a garden was in evidence. Noramary, who loved flowers dearly, was dismayed.

She had to remind herself quickly that Montclair had only recently been completed, and it still bore the stark look of newness. There had not been time enough to acquire the gracious patina of the older manor houses along the James River. Neither had there been Flemish masters to design intricate brick-work, nor landscape artists to plan formal gardens with Italian statuary. As Duncan had told her earlier, he himself had done much of the planning of the house.

And, in a way, the house reflected the man. Those qualities she had began to observe in him were an integral part of the building before her—honesty, simplicity, a certain quality of reserve and dignity. All it lacked was warmth.

In time, that could change. Perhaps all the house needed was someone to bring it charm, vitality, a personality uniquely its own. Perhaps she, as its mistress, could do just that.

And, of course, the setting was beautiful. *If only it weren't so isolated,* she thought. She gazed toward the house. But then Noramary's natural optimism rallied, for she had a child's heart, eager, expectant of good, hopeful of joy.

As they neared the house, a chill crept into the air. There was the smell of woodsmoke, and, somewhere in the distance, Noramary heard the harsh cawing of rooks. As she leaned out the carriage window, she saw several black menservants emerging from a side door, and a group of fine hunting dogs running alongside Duncan's horse, barking.

Then, finally, the carriage came to a stop, and a moment later Duncan opened the door and held out his hand to help her out. Noramary started to adjust her hood and gather her skirt to descend when she saw, over Duncan's broad shoulder, the front door opening and a tall woman in black stepped out onto the porch.

Instinctively Noramary drew back. A terrible feeling of dread swept over her. Her throat tightened. Without warning an unbidden thought formed in her mind, each word unmistakably clear: "In this house you will know your greatest happiness and your deepest sorrow."

Then Duncan's voice, warm and encouraging, broke into her moment of reverie. "Come, Noramary, we are here at last—at Montclair!"

Struggling not to reveal her sudden chilling experience, Noramary put her hand in his, at the same time calling to mind a passage of Scripture Nanny Oates had insisted she commit to memory before she left England: "Take courage, therefore, and be valiant. Fear not and be not dismayed: because the Lord thy God is with thee in all things whatsoever thou shalt go to."

Part II

He who finds a good wife finds a good thing and obtains favor from the Lord.

Proverbs 18:22

CHAPTER 11

JANET MONTROSE MCLEOD stepped onto the broad porch of Montclair, shivering in the chill wind that whipped her fine worsted shawl around her thin shoulders. She watched the arrival of the carriage bearing her brother's bride with mixed feelings of relief and some cautious expectation.

Relief, because she was anxious to return to her own home in Scotland. She had only come to Virginia in the first place to help her brother ready his new home for his bride, bringing with her some of their mother's silver, china and furniture that had come to her as the only daughter in the family at her mother's death. She wouldn't be needing them herself, for she was the widow of a prosperous Scot and had a country house full of his family's antiques and other fine furnishings.

She had never meant to stay this long. Janet disliked the erratic Virginia climate she remembered from her own childhood here. The humid summers, the damp winters, even the blindingly beautiful spring and the lush brilliance of autumn were not compensation enough. She longed for the Scottish coastal weather and the heather blue hills. If it had not been for the scandalous behavior of the other Barnwell girl, she would not have remained these many months.

Watching her brother dismount, Janet thought how handsome Duncan was, what a splendid man. Lucky girl, this Noramary Marsh, and it was profoundly to be hoped, she was of some finer and more honorable character than her fly-by-night cousin. Janet had been strongly opposed to Duncan's agreeing to marry into the same family. Blood will tell, she brooded. Likely as not, one girl was as flighty as the other. She had shaken her head and set her mouth in a tight line when Duncan had tried to tell her that Noramary was different. In the end Janet had said nothing. After all, her brother was twenty-nine, and if he were ever to take a bride, it must be soon. Here, in this part of Virginia, still verging on wilderness, a man needed a wife, companionship, warmth, and if he were lucky, affection . . . not that that always came with marriage, as Janet herself well knew.

Janet had hoped her brother would marry a woman trained and capable of taking over quickly. When she had seen Noramary's miniature, however, she had put those hopes aside. A mere child, if the pictures were any proof. And when she questioned Duncan he had told her, albeit reluctantly, that the girl was "barely seventeen." *Humph!* Janet snorted to herself. *Barely out of the schoolroom!*

With any luck the new Mrs. Montrose would be a fast learner. There was much to managing such a large plantation house. Its mistress had many duties other than presiding at a teatable, which was rumored to be all the young ladies in Williamsburg were taught. But Janet, ever one to do her duty, was determined to teach Noramary everything she needed to know before she departed.

Duncan had opened the carriage door and was

handing the girl out carefully. Her blue-lined hood had fallen back, and dark curls tumbled on either side of a delicate oval face. A tremulous smile turned up the corners of a full, sweet mouth. For all her glowing youth, Janet thought she looked fragile and felt a momentary foreboding. Would this delicate young girl be capable of shouldering the responsibilities of mistress of Montclair, physically strong enough to survive the demands of this isolated life and to bear the children Duncan so wanted, willing to sacrifice to build a family here on the edge of the wilderness?

But repressing her serious doubts, Janet hastened forward to welcome her new sister-in-law as Duncan led her up the steps.

"Welcome to Montclair, my dear," she said. "I am sorry not to have been able to attend your wedding, but I am, as you see, still in mourning for my dear husband." Turning to Duncan, she greeted him with a smile. "Come inside. You must be tired and hungry."

Duncan's sister was a very handsome woman, her features much like his, though cast in a feminine mold. Her lips were drawn more tightly, but her eyes were as keenly penetrating and kind. Her hair, the same russet brown as her brother's, was covered by a black lace widow's cap.

Pleasantly surprised by the genuine warmth of Janet's greeting, so different from that suggested by her stern appearance, Noramary stepped into the wide center hall. In contrast to the rather forbidding austerity of the outside, the interior of the house was cheerful and inviting. The wide-planked oak floors were highly polished and reflected the glow from a dozen candles burning in two wide-branched brass chandeliers. From the hall, Noramary could see through an arched doorway into the parlor, where an open fire in the wide hearth was burning brightly.

"This is Ellen, my housekeeper, who has been helping me with the preparations for your arrival."

Janet acknowledged the spare, sharp-featured woman who stepped forward and bowed slightly. She was wearing a gray dress, starchly collared, and a ruffled mobcap over carrot-colored hair.

"Mistress Montrose," she nodded, and Noramary started at the sound of her new title.

"And these are the house-servants," Duncan said. One by one, two shyly smiling black women, wearing blue homespun with starched aprons and colorful turbans, came forward and made an awkward curtsy, followed by two black men in white pleated shirts and black breeches. "Delva, Maysie, Thomas, Jason," Duncan introduced them.

"Would you like to see the house now?" Duncan asked Noramary with unconcealed eagerness.

Before she could answer him, Janet interjected, "Perhaps Noramary would first like to go to her room and freshen up after her long journey."

Suddenly conscious of her untidy appearance, Noramary put her hand to her hair and murmured, "Yes, perhaps that would be best. Thank you."

"Then we can have a nice tea," Janet said briskly.

"Forgive me, my dear. I wasn't thinking of your comfort. There will be plenty of time to see Montclair."

"Come along then," Janet nodded and, turning to one of the women, directed, "Delva, go and fetch Mistress Montrose some hot water and fresh linens."

Noramary bowed slightly to Duncan, then followed his sister's tall figure across the wide hallway. Janet opened the first door to the right, then stepped back to allow Noramary to proceed her into a large, high-ceilinged room.

If this room had been especially planned with her own tastes and comfort in mind, it could not have suited her more perfectly, Noramary marveled. In front of the fireplace, where a cheerful fire crackled, were two wing-backed chairs covered in crewel-embroidered linen and flanked by candlestands.

The windows were recessed, curtained in indigo blue, with cushioned seats. Before one of the windows was a small curved desk and chair, and against the opposite wall, a dainty dressing table with a tilted mirror and toilette box on top. An enormous tester bed with blue and white hangings and a quilted coverlet occupied the most prominent space.

"What a lovely room!" Noramary exclaimed.

"I'm glad you're pleased. Duncan had it completely repainted, the draperies and bed curtains changed after your cousin . . ." Janet halted abruptly. "Forgive me, Noramary. I just meant to say that Duncan wanted it done over in colors he felt would be more to your liking."

Duncan's thoughtfulness removed the sting of the reference to Winnie and the implication that the master bedroom had been originally planned to suit the tastes of another bride. It was a relief to Noramary that her room at Montclair was not simply another "hand-me-down."

Noramary blushed shyly and to cover her confusion moved over to one of the two other doors in the room. "Where do these lead?"

"That one is to Duncan's dressing room; the other, to your own, but there is another door inside. Why don't you see for yourself where that one leads?" Janet suggested.

Noramary walked into the dressing room equipped with a slipper chair and large armoire and then pushed open the small inner door to reveal a narrow winding staircase. She turned questioningly to Janet who stood at the door watching her.

"In the plans for the original house, this stairway led to our nursery. This plan gave the mother privacy and easy access to the child, and also the baby's nurse could come and go through the central hall without disturbing the parents. A very convenient arrangement, don't you see?"

Noramary nodded in agreement, though she felt that her limited experience in this area didn't qualify her for comment.

"Here comes Delva now with your water and towels, so I'll leave you. Tea will be served promptly in a half hour." Janet swept out of the room, closing the door behind her.

The tall, slim black girl approached Noramary, her delight in having been chosen to serve the new mistress, undisguised.

Noramary tied back her hair and washed herself, enjoying the refreshing sensation of the warm water and fine lavender-scented soap. She changed into fresh linens, relieved to be out of the blue woolsey traveling costume she had worn for the past twenty-four hours. Delva helped her into a cinnamon-colored bodice and gold overskirt looped in velvet ribbon, then helped arrange Noramary's hair in a shiny fall of rippling waves and secured it with a velvet ribbon.

When at last she joined Janet and Duncan in the parlor, she found an abundant teatable. Duncan, freshly changed, viewed her approvingly and, lifting the glass he was holding, said, "To your first day at Montclair, Noramary. May it be only the beginning of a lifetime of happiness under its roof."

At Duncan's words, she was reminded of the moment before she had stepped out of the carriage, when she had been gripped by a strange premonition. Nevertheless, she quickly banished it and, lifting her chin, acknowledged Duncan's toast.

"I pray God it will be so."

CHAPTER 12

A BLUE HAZE OF EARLY AUTUMN hung in the stillness of the afternoon as Noramary left the house. Once out of view she picked up her skirts and ran lightly along the woodland path. The crispness in the air was exhilarating, and the feeling of freedom from Janet's constant supervision, intoxicating. Noramary ran until she was breathless. On this particular afternoon Janet had retired for a nap—an event unprecedented in the three weeks Noramary had been at Montclair. The nap was in preparation for the long festive evening ahead, a farewell party given in Janet's honor. And though the two women had gotten on admirably, Noramary could not truly say she was sorry to see her go.

The next day Janet would depart for Yorktown, there to embark her ship for her return to Scotland. Ever since Noramary's arrival at Montclair, Janet had been instructing her on her duties as mistress. Contrary to Janet's fears and to her own astonishment, Noramary had been an apt pupil and had learned quickly.

These had been intense weeks, each day filled with learning, adjusting, absorbing all Janet was trying to teach her about the management of a huge plantation house. There had been a constant flow of callers, Duncan's neighbors, if one could call them such, separated as they were by great distances and hundreds of acres. Nevertheless, everyone had been eager to meet Duncan's bride, the new Mistress of Montclair.

And tonight would be her first time to entertain them officially in her new role, Noramary thought, half in anticipation, half in apprehension.

Noramary had learned, however, that being mistress of such a large manor house was much more complicated than playing the gracious hostess. It was a role she had never imagined would be so demanding. At first Noramary had been nearly overwhelmed by the duties detailed by her new sister-in-law: overseeing the houseservants, fourteen in all, each with different duties to supervise.

Daily, there was the cleaning, dusting, waxing, and polishing required to keep the twenty-room house sparkling. There were menus to discuss with the cook, then supplies to be measured and brought from the storehouses; the available fruits and vegetables in season, to be picked from the gardens and orchards. Since all the fabric for the servants' clothing was processed on the plantation, there was the supervision of wool-carding, spinning, dying, and weaving. The linen for bedding and table use was made from flax grown on the land.

Since candle-dipping and soap-making were important to the smooth operation of the household, the mistress must keep close check on the progress of these activities so that supplies never ran short.

It seemed there was no end to the list of responsibilities Noramary would assume upon Janet's departure. The very thought of it left her dizzy. The Barnwell household, with fewer servants, had seemed to run itself. Now, however, Noramary realized that was probably due to Aunt Betsy's efficient management and the training she had given all four girls.

At the end of the first few days, following Janet as she made rounds, Noramary was nearing exhaustion. She found she could barely keep her eyes open throughout the late dinner hour and fell asleep the instant her head touched the pillow each night.

Guiltily, Noramary knew she would not miss her sister-in-law's cold, patrician face, the fastidious manners, the tedious way she had of explaining things. Nevertheless, Janet's efficiency and swift dispatch of duty would leave a gaping void.

Thank God for Ellen, Noramary thought gratefully.

It had been decided that Janet's own housekeeper, Ellen Anderson, whom she had brought with her to Virginia, would stay awhile longer to assist Noramary.

Noramary liked Ellen, who was bright and cheerful, with an unexpected and delightful sense of humor. Most importantly, the brisk Scotswoman was wonderfully proficient in all the household tasks.

By the time Noramary reached the rustic bridge spanning the creek, she was breathless, both from her brisk run and from her turbulent thoughts. Since the night she and Duncan had been stranded by the flash flood, the little bridge had been repaired. She paused, leaning on the rail, and looked down to the sun-dappled water rushing over the rocks and swirling into opalescent eddies. She had had no time to herself for weeks and now she felt a sudden, heart-catching loneliness.

These had been strange weeks since her arrival on that stormy night. Strangest of all, perhaps, was her puzzling relationship with her new husband. Husband? Perhaps not, for they were not yet husband and wife in the fullest sense, and she was puzzled why that was so.

Her very first night at Montclair, he had escorted her to the master suite. There he had bowed over her hand, kissed it, and told her gravely that, after his two-week absence, there were plantation records that needed reviewing. He bade her good night and a pleasant rest, and left her staring after him in bewilderment.

The next morning when she had awakened in the bed alone her curiosity piqued, she had tiptoed over to the dressing room door and looked in. The room was empty. There was evidence, however, that Duncan had slept on the narrow couch in the recessed alcove.

Since then, he had continued to sleep in the adjoining dressing room. Duncan seemed fond of her, was unfailingly courteous, seemed ever interested in providing her with any number of things for her pleasure and happiness. With eager pride he had shown her the music room where a small harpsichord stood waiting. No doubt he had purchased it especially for her after hearing her play, for Winnie was not musical. On another occasion he had taken her out to the stables and presented her with the gift of a gentle, sweet-tempered black mare.

"She's yours to name," Duncan had said, smiling down at her.

"Cinders" had become a delight and a welcome respite on several mornings when Noramary managed to escape Janet's relentless tutelage.

Though Noramary was innocent, as were most of the other unmarried young women of her acquaintance, still she was troubled. Surely by this time her marriage to Duncan should be more than affectionate consideration and lavish gifts.

Of course, there were doubtless many practical reasons for his frequent absences. This was harvest time at Montclair, and Duncan spent long days in the saddle, riding over the acres and acres of land, while her days were crowded as well. And then there was Janet's constant presence—at meals, in the parlor, in the kitchen, wherever Noramary turned. There was little opportunity for romantic intimacy with her husband under these unusual circumstances.

Fleetingly Noramary recalled those few hours of laughter and unique camaraderie she and Duncan had shared so unpredictably on their wedding night in the warmth of the little cottage. Perhaps . . . after Janet was gone . . . Noramary mused.

Noramary stretched out her hand, surveying the ring on her finger alongside her wedding band. Only that morning Janet had called her upstairs to the room she had been occupying while at Montclair. Her trunks were open, and she was doing the last of her packing. Noramary had expected some last-minute instructions. Instead, Janet had taken off a large ring from her own finger and handed it to Noramary.

"This is the traditional Montrose betrothal ring," she explained. "It came to me upon our mother's death. But I think you should have it, wear it, as the first Mistress of Montclair."

Noramary had often noticed the dark purple amethyst on Janet's finger, but had never examined it closely. Now, as it lay in her palm, she saw its exquisite craftsmanship, the stone in a heart-shaped setting, held by two sculptured hands under a tiny crown.

"It's very lovely, Janet. Are you sure I should have it?"

"I have no sons to inherit it," Janet said firmly. "And it is my belief that it should stay in the Montrose family to be handed on to your son to give to his wife, then down through the family."

To your son . . . Janet's words came to her now as she held out her hand, turning the ring this way and that to catch the sun and split its rays into a million lavender lights.

Noramary left the bridge and walked on, still lost in thought. She came to a clearing in the woods and there, on a little rise, she saw the little cottage where she and Duncan had stayed the night of the storm. Something real, something tender and strong had sprung up between them; a bond had been forged, tenuous perhaps, but in it there had been an unspoken promise given, but not yet fulfilled.

She stood there for awhile, looking at the small house nestled in the trees, then she turned and started slowly back along the path leading to Montclair. Perhaps Duncan was waiting for some sign from her—that she was willing at last to make their marriage a true union. Maybe, just maybe, it was up to her. . . .

Tonight would present her first opportunity to show him that, even though she had not been his first choice, she was the right choice.

Tonight she would make Duncan Montrose proud, happy that she had become his bride—even if the substitute bride.

CHAPTER 13

SEATED AT HER DRESSING TABLE Noramary, brush in hand, considered the possibility of letting Delva powder her hair for the evening's festivities.

The candles in the sconces on either side of the mirror cast flattering light, reflecting her serious expression as she weighed her decision. Delva, anxiously awaiting her mistress's directions, stood behind with the horn-shaped paper face mask and powder bowl, ready to dust Noramary's rich dark hair if she was directed.

"No," said Noramary finally, "it's much too much bother." *Besides*, she thought, *Duncan never powders his hair, even for formal occasions*. And tonight, standing by his side to receive their guests, she wanted to complement him.

"Now, Delva, if you'll put that messy stuff away, you can help me with my gown."

Noramary stood while the girl carefully dropped the damask underskirt over her head and tied it in the back. With the width of the three starched muslin petticoats Noramary was wearing, her tiny waist looked even smaller. Then the puffed taffeta paniers were attached, adding more fashionable breadth. Next came the shirred satin bodice with the tiny buttons to be fastened down the back. Stiff lace ruffled the square neckline and elbow-length sleeves.

"Oh, ma'am, yo' does look mos' beautiful! Jes' wait 'til Marster Duncan sees yo'." Delva stepped back, smiling, head cocked to one side in admiration.

Noramary surveyed herself critically, thinking with some satisfaction that, although this modish creation was also one of those hand-me-downs made for Winnie's trousseau, then altered for Noramary's taller, more slender figure, it was extremely becoming. It was blue the color of a peacock's feather, chosen to enhance Winnie's blonde prettiness. Nonetheless, the gown proved spectacular with Noramary's vivid blue eyes and high coloring.

Her second thought was her hope that Duncan would be pleased with her appearance. She had seen him ride in from his field inspection earlier. From her window she had watched as he swung himself out of the saddle, moving with careless grace, then took the steps into the house, two at a time. A little later she had heard his voice mingled with that of his man servant's from the dressing room and knew he, too, was getting ready for the evening.

Noramary felt an excited little tingle at the prospect of her role as hostess for the evening. Many times she had helped Aunt Betsy entertain guests, but never before had she enjoyed the privilege of overseeing an elegant party in her own magnificent home.

Even as she was thinking these thoughts, a knock from Duncan's dressing room door startled her and she turned just as he entered the bedroom, handsome in a saffron satin coat, fluted neckpiece and cuffs, creamy breeches.

"Good evening, Noramary," he said, his sweeping glance taking note of every detail. "How truly lovely you look."

The spontaneous compliment seemed to surprise him as much as it pleased Noramary, for he reddened slightly under his tan. Then, as if to cover his own unaccustomed shyness, he took a few steps toward her, extending a rectangular velvet jewel case.

"I'd be pleased if you'd wear these tonight. They belonged to my mother." He pressed the spring lock, and the lid snapped open to reveal a magnificent ruby brooch surrounded by diamonds and a set of matching earrings of teardrop-shaped rubies, also surrounded by tiny diamonds.

"Oh, Duncan, they're exquisite!"

"There is a gold chain so that you can also wear the brooch as a pendant if you'd prefer," Duncan explained. "Here." He handed her the box.

She lifted them carefully from the box, fastened in the earrings, then turned to Duncan, holding out the fragile chain on which she had attached the brooch.

"Will you fasten the clasp for me?" she asked. With one hand she lifted her curls and bent her slender neck. As his fingers touched her bare skin, she felt a little shiver. When he had secured the catch, his hands moved tentatively along her neck to her shoulders, lingering there for a moment. She spun slowly around to face him.

"I'm afraid you and Janet are spoiling me," she teased. "Why only today she gave me this—another Montrose jewel." She held out her hand so he could see the betrothal ring. "With all these family treasures, I am truly beginning to feel like your wife!"

The minute the words were out of her mouth, she regretted them. But Duncan's eyes seemed to blaze with sudden fire, and then he caught both her hands and brought them to his lips.

"Not quite, Noramary," he said huskily. "There is something important I want to say to you—that I've meant to tell you for some time. But there hasn't been the opportunity . . . nor could I find the words." He paused, struggling to go on.

Duncan was gazing at her with such tenderness that Noramary felt a warm melting sensation. Meeting those clear gray eyes, she experienced a sense of intimate communion between them. Then Duncan spoke again.

"No matter how it came about, I am so very happy you agreed to become my wife. The rubies were my father's wedding present to my mother and have come to be called the Montrose Bridal Set." He paused again, then his voice grew hoarse with emotion. "Noramary, from the moment I met you, I felt—even then—something different. I think . . . I believe I have been waiting for you all these years."

"Well, here I am," she replied softly.

Her lovely eyes seemed to reflect the shining thing suspended between them, fragile as a butterfly wing, a silken thread that might, in time, become a strong, sure bond.

At that very moment an insistent tapping came upon their bedroom door, and Janet's piercing voice intruded.

"Duncan, Noramary, a carriage is coming up the drive. Your guests are arriving!"

Duncan groaned under his breath, sighed heavily, and smiled—a smile that did unexpected things to Noramary's heart.

"Later . . ." he whispered. "When everyone is gone . . ." The implication dangled as he drew her to him, framed her face in his hands, and bent to kiss her. Her lips yielded sweetly to his kiss, and it left her strangely stirred.

"Come, Mistress Montrose. Our guests are waiting." He took Noramary's hand and slipped it through his arm. "There will be time for us . . . we have a whole lifetime ahead of us."

The evening was a gaily festive one. Virginians in this part of the country knew how to enjoy themselves, Noramary discovered, finding the company as cultured, the conversation as spritely, the ladies as elegantly gowned, the gentlemen as suave as any she had observed in Williamsburg circles.

Throughout the evening she kept glancing at Duncan, thinking of the unforeseen intimacy of their earlier encounter, his eloquent declaration. Noramary was deeply moved to know he had cared for her so long ago. Duncan, she was learning, was a man of many moods, an intriguing, fascinating man.

With renewed resolution, Noramary determined to put the past behind her forever, and, not even by a random thought, betray the trust and honor this good and gracious man had given her. She would be to Duncan Montrose the best wife it was in her ability to be—with God's help!

The Camerons had brought with them their house-guest, Cecil Brandon, a well-known English artist who had been commissioned by James to paint the portraits of Jacqueline and their two young sons, Bracken and Brett.

He was now bending over Noramary's hand after their introduction, and, when he straightened, she could feel his practiced eye appraising her. If she could have read his thoughts, she would been quite overwhelmed.

What an exquisite creature. And how incredible to find such a vision in this vast wilderness. Of course, Jacqueline Cameron is a great beauty, but it is to be expected. She is from France—a sophisticated, worldly woman. On the other hand, Mistress Montrose is hardly more than a girl, with the radiant innocence of childhood still upon her—the heart-shaped face, the delicate ivory skin, the magnificent violet eyes, slender figure, cloud of dark hair . . . entrancing!

All through dinner Brandon could not take his eyes from her, while all around him the conversation flowed almost unheeded.

Even though Noramary was unaware of his observation, it did not escape the notice of Jacqueline and
Duncan. They exchanged a knowing glance, then
Duncan himself followed the direction of the artist's
focus and smiled, joyful that this treasure belonged to
him.

Indeed, Noramary did look lovely in the mellow
candleglow, Duncan thought, the gleam of her dark
hair pulled high, exposing her tiny ears with the
bobbing flash of the ruby earrings and the creamy
expanse of throat and shoulder. She seemed to him
even more beautiful than the first time he had met her.
How strangely things had turned out! Duncan recalled
his bitter frustration after that first meeting at the
Barnwells' party, the despair when he realized he had
met Noramary too late—that he was already engaged
to her cousin!

As he looked down the table-length, he could hardly
believe his good fortune. A man might wonder if there
really were a planned purpose for life . . . if he and
Noramary had really been destined for each other,
after all.

Suddenly Noramary caught his glance and smiled at
him. Hope leaped afresh in Duncan's heart. He and
this woman *would* build a wonderful life together at
Montclair. What had once seemed a vague dream now
appeared to be reality. Duncan could not believe his
good fortune!

Brandon impatiently endured the traditional ritual
of brandy and conversation among the men when the
ladies withdrew after dinner. However, as soon as
they rejoined them in the drawing room, Brandon
sought out Noramary immediately.

"Madam, I must compliment you on the delicious
dinner, the beautifully appointed table. I cannot
remember when I have enjoyed a gathering more," he
began. Then, unable to contain his enthusiasm, he

blurted out, "Madam, I must paint you . . . if you would permit it."

Noramary was completely taken aback. Then, as if by appointment, Duncan was beside her and Brandon was directing his request to her husband.

"Sir, I would like very much to paint a portrait of your wife. Indeed, I would consider it a privilege to do so."

Noramary turned to Duncan and was surprised to see the look of pleasure and pride in his expression.

"I see you appreciate beauty, sir," he said.

"Beauty, yes, but not just beauty for itself, sir. Only when it is coupled with an inner sweetness of soul, unspoiled and pristine . . . that is when I want to capture it . . . before it is corrupted in any way." He made a slight gesture to Noramary. "As this lady can surely testify, too much beauty can be a burden . . . unless it brings peace, tranquility and happiness."

Noramary made a small movement as if in protest to Brandon's extravagant phrases, yet at the same time she was moved by his perception. Had she not felt the weight of just such a burden when, even as a child of twelve, that stunning, sensitive beauty had caused her heartbreak?

Then Duncan was speaking. "Perhaps when I return from accompanying my sister to board her ship in Yorktown, we can make some arrangements about having Noramary's portrait done. How long do you expect to be in this part of the country?"

Noramary did not absorb much of the rest of their conversation; she was too bemused by Duncan's eagerness to comply with Brandon's suggestion. She was even more aware that while they had been talking to the artist, Duncan's arm had circled her waist, its gentle pressure sending a tremor of pleasure through her.

Finally the evening came to an end. The guests began to leave, with many thanks, return invitations and promises to visit, as well as farewells and Godspeed to Janet.

As was his custom, Duncan rode to the gates alongside the carriages of his departing guests. Janet, pleading weariness and need for sleep before her long journey the next day, took her candle and retired.

Noramary lingered, walking back into the dining room, admiring once again the elegant table, flowers and candlelabra still in place. Then she wandered into the drawing room, feeling a new pride in its handsome furnishings, the quiet dignity of its atmosphere. This was her home now. She was mistress here. And, to her amazement, she had enjoyed her role as hostess more than she had imagined possible. Duncan, too, had seemed pleased.

What an evening it had been! She had felt more like herself than at any time since . . . well, since long before she had left Williamsburg. It was as if some heavy weight had fallen away and she could now take a long breath without pain.

Was it possible that something had transpired between herself and Duncan tonight that bode well for their relationship? Could the growing respect and affection she had for him be turning to love? Did such things really happen?

Tonight they had seemed a real couple. She recalled how, arm in arm, they had moved among their guests before dinner, stopping to chat with this group and that. Noramary had felt relaxed, and Duncan had seemed to take delight in her every word. She had found it easy and natural to visit with Duncan's friends, even to bringing off a bit of humor now and then. Later, at dinner, she could feel Duncan's eyes upon her from his place at the opposite end of the table, and she had experienced an instantaneous rush of pleasure. Something intangible tingled in that silent communication, something that made her pulses race, brought flaming color to her cheeks, set her heart beating so fast that it was hard to breathe.

Delva was waiting for Noramary in the bedroom. But after she had helped her mistress out of her elaborate gown and into her blue panné velvet peignoir, Noramary sent the girl away.

Thoughtfully Noramary replaced the rubies in their case. The Monrose Bridal Set. Her hand stroked the velvet lid, remembering the poignant moment when Duncan had given them to her. The promise in his eyes when he had kissed her. Would this be the night she would truly become his wife?

Noramary looked at the high, canopied bed, its silken coverlet turned back invitingly, the mounds of ruffled pillows offering peaceful repose. But Noramary was far too stimulated by the events of the evening to be sleepy.

She brushed her hair, giving it long, vigorous strokes until it crackled. She sat for a long moment, regarding herself in the mirror with a kind of curiosity. What had Brandon seen in her face that compelled him to paint her portrait? And why had Duncan acquiesced so readily?

Sighing, she blew out her candle, crossed to the window, thrust it open and leaned on the sill, looking out into the night.

The air was cold, with the snap of autumn; the moon glistened on the early frost that coated the grass and outlined the tender saplings Duncan had planted along the drive.

Duncan! A little tingle coursed through Noramary. How long would it take him to ride to the gate with the last guests . . . and return?

CHAPTER 14

DAWN'S FAINT BLUSH stained the pale gray morning with shimmering light and gradually stole into the master bedroom at Montclair.

Duncan leaned down to kiss Noramary's eyelids, still closed in sleep, and gently brushed back the dark strands of silky hair from her forehead. She stirred in his arms, half-waking.

"It's time to get up, dearest," he whispered regretfully. "Janet will be up and anxious to leave as soon as it's fully light."

At that Noramary's eyelids fluttered, then opened. She looked up into Duncan's face, and her eyes widened as if in surprise. Then, in a rather drowsy remembrance, a tiny smile turned up the corners of her rosy mouth and she sighed contentedly. As awareness sharpened, she recalled how infinitely tenderly Duncan had made her fully his wife.

That's what he had murmured over and over, *beloved wife*.

He gathered her close, and, as Noramary put her arms around his neck, he buried his head in her

107

sweetly scented hair. That she could return his love filled Duncan with a sense of gratitude and tenderness so sharp it was almost pain.

"I hate to leave you, my darling," Duncan said, releasing her reluctantly, "but I'll only be gone long enough to see Janet safely aboard her ship and settled. I'll be away only a few days."

Only a few days, Duncan had said, but as soon as Noramary saw the carriage disappear at the bend of the drive, she felt a strange emptiness. And as the days passed, she was amazed that she could miss him so much.

Of course, Noramary was not used to solitude. The Barnwell household had been a lively one, with four girls coming and going constantly, and a steady stream of company besides. It had been a home filled with noise, chatter, the sound of running feet, laughter.

Here, with only the houseservants for company, Noramary experienced an altogether new kind of loneliness. To her amusement she found she missed Janet as one would miss an aching tooth when it has been pulled! She was, however, more grateful than ever for her sister-in-law's rigorous instruction, for the household tasks filled many of the lonely hours and provided a welcome pattern to the days Duncan was away.

As the days of Duncan's expected return drew near, Noramary found herself anticipating his homecoming with equal portions of joy and reserve. Their intimate relationship was still so new, so tenuous, that she had to wonder if the days apart had changed him. She still did not know Duncan well, and Janet's warning came to mind.

They had been putting out the elaborate silver flatware that was to be polished for use at the dinner party. Pausing in the act of counting the place settings, Janet had spoken in a low, serious tone.

108

"I hope you will not misunderstand what I am about to say, Noramary. Please try to accept it as an older woman's advice to one just starting out in married life. I do not know how well you think you know my brother, but I feel I should give you fair warning.

"You have heard the saying, 'Still waters run deep,' haven't you? Well, that could have been written of my brother. On the surface, he may appear calm, controlled, but he is a complex man. A man of strong passions, of fierce loyalty, unswerving honor, lasting love. But I have also witnessed his anger, sudden, violent as summer lightning, followed by cold, implacable unforgiveness and ruthless retribution. I say this not to frighten you, but to warn you.

"You are very young, and the young sometimes act thoughtlessly, behave recklessly or take carelessly things that older people cherish or venerate. I would caution you to be aware of the fragile quality of most relationships . . . especially the one between a husband and wife."

Noramary had been tempted to pursue the conversation, to ask Janet about those times when she had seen Duncan's darker side, but something had kept her from doing so. Still, she could not help wondering if one of those times might have been when he learned of Winnie's elopement. Such an event could be devastating to a man's pride, fill him with feelings of anger, resentment, a desire for revenge. Yet, it was hard to picture the Duncan she had come to know as unforgiving. He seemed compassionate, understanding, gentle, as only a strong, confident man could be. Because Janet was not inclined to discuss the matter further, Noramary tucked the information in the back of her mind, hoping that she herself would never have to witness this terrifying anger of Duncan's or, worse still, be the cause of it.

From what Janet had said, Duncan certainly had

none of Robert's impulsive charm, boyish gaiety, mischievous sense of humor, Noramary thought, then quickly chided herself for making such a comparison.

She did not want to think of Robert, but in those long, lonely afternoons, when she walked alone through the autumn woods surrounding Montclair, thoughts of him came to her despite her resolution to thrust him forever out of her mind. They had often tramped in the woodlands near Williamsburg on just such lovely, golden, Indian summer days.

The nights during Duncan's absence were even more unmanageable. Even though she had fallen asleep only once in his embrace, the secure comfort she had felt within his arms now made it difficult to sleep soundly in the bed they had shared.

Each night he had been gone, Noramary had tossed and turned, then drifted into a shallow slumber, troubled by dreams. To her dismay, the dreams had been of Robert Stedd! Two mornings she had awakened with his name on her lips, shaken by memories she had thought long since banked.

Earnestly Noramary tried to discipline herself to keep her mind occupied.

Aunt Betsy had started her on a sampler when she had first come to Williamsburg. All the cousins were at work on similar projects, as it was deemed essential for all young ladies to display not only their skill with a needle, but to present the saga of their individual lives, ideals, and thoughts. Since coming to Montclair, however, Noramary had put aside this project to assume the demanding duties required of her as mistress.

Now she found that the evenings gave her time to take up her needlework again, and she had made good progress, even adding a line of Scripture to embroider at the bottom of the sampler.

On the morning of Duncan's expected return, Noramary rose early, eager to see that the servants were about their tasks. By early afternoon, she was dressed in one of the most flattering of her "at home" dresses, a coral wool bodice with a cream tucker and skirt embroidered with wild rowan berry blossoms.

Making a final inspection of the house, she noted with satisfaction and pride the polished perfection of each room. There were fires burning in all the fireplaces; the scent of candlewax and the fragrance of flowers mingled pungently with the smell of applewood logs. It was a bright and cheerful house—a house awaiting its master's return.

As the afternoon shadows lengthened, Noramary became more restive, frequently looking out the window to peer down the drive for some sign of the returning traveler.

At length she settled herself at her frame and diligently applied herself to her sampler, trying to suppress her nervousness. Her needle was poised over the canvas when she started at a sound outside. Carriage wheels? Yes, it was! Noramary flew to the window as the carriage rumbled into sight. Duncan—home at last!

She ran from the room and down the hall. But when she saw Titus, one of the houseservants, opening the front door, she halted, assuming the more dignified stance expected of the mistress.

She held her breath as Duncan stepped inside, handed his caped coat to Titus, and glanced past him to Noramary, standing in the archway to the drawing room. Seeing her, he beamed with pleasure.

"Welcome home, Duncan," she said demurely, dropping a little curtsy.

"It's good to be home," Duncan said heartily, his eyes feasting upon her until her cheeks flamed.

"Shall we serve dinner now, Mistress?" asked Titus.

Noramary glanced at Duncan with lifted eyebrows.

"In another half hour, Titus. Tell Cook," Duncan

ordered. "I want a few minutes with Mistress Mont-rose." Again his glance swept Noramary. "Let us go into the parlor, my dear. I have something to show you."

Tucking her arm through his, he led her through the arched doorway. Once inside, he cupped her chin with one hand and kissed her mouth lightly, then with his other hand, he drew a small package from his waistcoat pocket and handed it to her.

"A gift!" Noramary gave a cry of delight. "Oh, Duncan, you are spoiling me terribly!"

"Perhaps I like spoiling you," he said, smiling at her with great tenderness.

Noramary had received few presents in her life, and so it was with a child's eagerness that she opened the little box. When she lifted out a dainty folded fan, her face lighted up.

"Duncan, how lovely!"

With a flick of her wrist, she unfurled it, displaying the arch of creamy silk on which a spray of tiny red roses was handpainted. The sticks were of filigreed ivory, with a crimson satin tassel dancing from the guard. She held it up in front of her face in a coquettish gesture, fluttering it flirtatiously.

Duncan laughed at her nonsense. "I'm glad it pleases you. So then, what have you been doing with yourself while I've been gone?"

"For one thing, I've accomplished quite a bit on my sampler," Noramary announced much like a little girl reporting on her schoolwork. Still fluttering her new fan, she walked over to the frame and tapped it with her fingers. "It's almost finished."

"I shall have to examine it. I understand a sampler is supposed to be representative of a young lady's achievements in needlework as well as a revelation of her ideals, her thoughts, and her spiritual state." His voice held a teasing quality, although he maintained a serious expression.

"Come see for yourself!" Noramary challenged.

He walked over to the tapestry frame and with great solemnity appeared to be studying it carefully.

The sampler was uniquely the story of Noramary's life thus far. At the top she had outlined Monksmoor Priory, her childhood home, and the date of her birth. Coming to Virginia by ship had, at the time, been the single most important event in Noramary's life, so she had traced the "Fairwinds" in colorful yarn. Next she had added her rendition of the Barnwells' yellow clapboard house and a row of flowers, new to her, found in the garden there. All these had symbolized her new life in America. Most recently she had recorded other details since coming to Montclair. Now, only her signature remained to be stitched at the bottom. The letters in her name, NORAMARY MARSH, had been completed, and she had just begun to fill in the letters of her new married name—M O N T R O S E.

Duncan slowly read the words aloud, placing significant emphasis on the last name. He looked up and smiled. Then he continued, reading the Scripture verse she had worked on during the last week: "Delight thyself in the Lord; and he shall give thee the desires of thine heart—Psalm 37:4."

The candlelight softened the angular planes of his face as he regarded Noramary silently. "And what are the desires of your heart, Noramary?"

She gave him a level look, her eyes sweetly grave. "My heart's desire is to please God, Duncan, and you," she said at length, lowering her head so that he could not see into her eyes through the dark veil of her lashes. "To be your wife . . . in every sense of the word . . . to belong to you . . . really belong. That is the desire of my heart," knowing for the first time that it was really true.

Almost as if speaking to himself, he said, "That has been the desire of my heart, too."

At his words a sudden joy seized Noramary and tears sprang to her eyes. She saw something in Duncan's face she had never seen before, and she realized that he had never looked at anyone quite like he was gazing at her now.

If she were his second choice, the substitute of the bride he had desired, she no longer cared. At that moment the past seemed to fade away, and only the growing eagerness to love and be loved swelled in her heart.

She held out her arms to him, tenderness and expectation spreading through her in a warm, enveloping glory. He did not speak for a moment, then he drew her to him, enclosing her in his arms, his chin resting atop her silky head.

"Darling Noramary, you have made me happier than I ever dreamed possible."

Her slender body swayed closer and, sighing her name, he gathered her to him.

CHAPTER 15

AT DAYBREAK THE DISTANT sounds of birdsong broke the stillness. Pale light, filtering through the louvered shutters of the windows, banished the night shadows.

In the large canopy bed Duncan stirred and awakened, propping himself on one elbow to observe his still sleeping wife. He was not sure how long he had slept, nor what had disturbed his slumber, but something had roused him.

Just at that moment Noramary moved restlessly. Her head turned from side to side; a frown drew the smooth brow into a pucker, and her eyelids fluttered. Duncan leaned closer, but could not understand the words she was mumbling.

Poor darling, he thought. *Having a bad dream perhaps.* He touched her shoulder, gently pressing it. At his touch she uttered a few incoherent words, and with her eyes still closed, reached up and drew his head down against her breast.

Duncan's arms went around her, holding her close. "I'm here, darling," he whispered comfortingly. "Dearest Noramary, I love you."

115

Noramary smiled as if with some secret joy. "And I love you. . . ."

At the name she whispered, shock like a saber thrust pierced Duncan's heart. It reverberated in his brain, settled into his consciousness.

Robert! I love you, Robert! Robert?

Who was this Robert whose name Noramary had spoken with such passionate tenderness? Noramary, to whom he had opened himself with a surrender, an intensity he had never thought possible. Noramary, in whom all his inner loneliness had been assuaged. Noramary, with whom he had found an ecstasy beyond his wildest imagining. She had deceived him! She had dreamed of another man while in his—Duncan's—arms! *Robert.*

Stiffly he loosened Noramary's clinging arms, withdrew himself from her embrace and dragged himself from the bed. His hands clenched into fists as he stood staring down at her in a kind of disbelief that she could look so innocent—her dark hair, feathered out against the white linen pillow; her cheeks, flushed with sleep; her lips, slightly parted as if expecting to be kissed.

The blood roared in Duncan's temples; his heart thudded heavily; he felt as if he couldn't breathe. In his mouth he tasted the bitter gall of disillusionment. How quickly their joy had turned into a kind of heartsick despair.

He dragged on his clothes, moving wearily, like a man twice his age. He pulled on his boots and walked over to the fireplace. The fire that had glowed so brightly when he and Noramary had entered the bedroom the night before was now a heap of crumbled logs, mostly ashes. Like his own hopes and dreams, he thought dully.

Duncan felt a tremor of suppressed fury course through his veins.

How could he have been so deceived? So taken in by her naïveté? What a clever actress, how devious.

He thought of their courtship during the summer just past, how restrained he had behaved with her, never taking the slightest advantage, afraid he might importune her delicate nature, frighten her if he revealed the depth of his love and desire for her.

And all the while, perhaps even up until the wedding day, she had been seeing, perhaps carrying on a clandestine affair with this—this Robert, whose name she had uttered with such tenderness. Duncan felt cheated, betrayed by his own emotions as well as the falseness of the one to whom he had allowed himself to be so vulnerable.

More fool he! And what was God's design for them now?

Duncan put on his jacket, searched for his neck-piece which he had carelessly dropped somewhere last night in his haste. As he moved about, he stumbled against the small candle table and set it to rocking noisily.

Noramary awakened. Coming slowly out of a happy dream of childhood days, she raised herself on her elbows and looked around drowsily. Still half-asleep, she was smiling, for her dream had been the first one for months not plagued with sad memories or vain regrets. She had dreamed of the days when she and Robert had played together, along with the Barnwell girls—a time when they had all been young, carefree, unburdened.

Seeing Duncan, Noramary felt the newly awakened love for him like an embracing warmth.

"Duncan," she called, sitting up and holding out her arms to him.

Duncan whirled around, steeling himself not to succumb at the sight of her—the tumbled dark waves falling about her sleep-rosy face, the smile trembling on her lips.

"Duncan?"

This time it was a tentative appeal, her eyes

widened, taking in his fixed look. She shivered involuntarily and huddled under the covers, drawing them up to her chin. "What is it, Duncan? Is something the matter?"

Noramary waited for him to speak. When Duncan made no move toward her, she remained poised in a questioning attitude, trying to read the cold anger his eyes seemed to hold.

What could she possibly have done to deserve that look of withering scorn? Noramary searched his face, seeking some reassurance for the sudden coldness she saw in his eyes.

The chilling silence was finally broken when Duncan, visibly suppressing rage, spoke in a toneless voice.

"I have only a few things to say to you, madam, and they are of immense importance. First, I believe we can both agree that I never importuned you nor unduly pressured you to consummate our marriage."

An unknown fear gripped Noramary as, bewildered, she waited for Duncan to continue even as she dreaded hearing what he was going to say.

"Whatever you chose not to reveal to me before our marriage was your privilege. However, it is inexcusable that you would pretend a passion you did not feel, when there was another man in your life. You have profaned the vows we took together, vows which I held sacred.

"It was clearly understood by me that you entered into this marriage of your own free will, under no duress from me or your aunt and uncle. Now I have reason to believe that I have been doubly deceived."

Noramary started to protest, but he cut her short with his next words. "But we have made a commitment, you and I, a pledge, promises made before God and witnesses. These shall remain. As far as the rest of the world is concerned, we are pledged to each other for life. I shall never break that bond. You are my wife and shall always be, but . . . our marriage will be in fact what it has become, a mere façade; in reality, the sham *you* have made it.''

His voice was harsh and cruel, and the mouth that had lingered so lovingly on hers twisted into a hard line.

With that, Duncan turned and stalked toward the door.

Noramary, who had been paralyzed by the flood of Duncan's angry words, threw back the covers and jumped out of bed, running after him on bare feet. Recklessly, she grabbed hold of his sleeve.

''Wait! Duncan, wait!'' she pleaded. ''I don't understand. What have I done? Why are you so angry with me?''

''For God's sake, Noramary . . .'' He paused significantly. ''Yes . . . for God's sake, and mine, please don't make it any worse!''

He shook off her clutching hands and strode out of the room without a backward glance.

Part III

Wrath is cruel, and anger is outrageous; but who is able to stand before envy? Open rebuke is better than secret love.

Proverbs 27:4,5

CHAPTER 16

FOR WEEKS AFTERWARD, Noramary relived that dreadful scene, and the one that took place later that same evening. Neither seemed real to her.

When Duncan had stormed out of the bedroom, leaving her in anguished bewilderment, Noramary had collapsed in spasms of uncontrollable weeping. What had she said, what had she done to deserve Duncan's heartless rejection?

All her new happiness, the joy he had awakened in her at the sweetness of his embrace was replaced with a numbing emptiness. That beautiful flame that had touched both of them and burned so brightly, yet so briefly, between them was gone. Destroyed by some reason known only to Duncan.

The rest of that day she had wandered about the house as if in a trance, waiting miserably for Duncan's return from the fields. She awaited only the chance to plead with him again for an explanation.

But when he had walked into the house, he had given her only a cold glance and walked straight into the drawing room without greeting her.

She followed him, saying humbly, "Duncan, we must talk."

"Well?" Duncan demanded impatiently. "What do we have to talk about?"

"Please," she said in a low voice, "I do not care to be overheard." Noramary inclined her head slightly toward the dining room where the maids were setting the table for dinner.

"Very well. Come in then."

She entered the parlor, closing the French doors behind her. He stood facing her, slapping his riding gloves smartly on his palm, a frown on his face. His whole demeanor intimidated her, but she was too desperate not to attempt some understanding.

She lifted her head bravely, determined to see this through, and asked as quietly and calmly as she could manage, "Duncan, I must know what I have done to anger you so. How can I apologize if I don't know . . ."

But he interrupted her, "I thought I made myself clear this morning. I have nothing more to say. The subject is distasteful in the extreme to me, and I will not discuss it further."

Rebuffed, Noramary struggled not to lose her composure. But when she spoke, her voice betrayed her emotion. "If you will not give me the chance to defend myself, what is there for me to do? There is nothing left for me to think but that you deeply regret the agreement you made with my aunt and uncle to marry me, that you desperately wish you'd never accepted a substitute bride."

Saying that, Noramary turned to leave, intent on hiding the tears in her eyes.

"One moment, madam." His harsh command halted her as her hand touched the door handle. "I will be gone most of the time for the next ten days or so. The tobacco crop is being harvested and I must oversee its cutting, drying and tying at the other end of the plantation. So, do not expect me for dinner in the evenings. If I should come, have my meal served on a tray in the office."

Her back still to him, Noramary asked, "Is that all then?"

"One thing more, madam. You may rest assured that I will never again assume my so-called marital rights. As far as I am concerned, we live under this roof as man and wife—in name only."

Noramary, biting back the tears that threatened to blind her, opened the double doors and, holding herself erect, walked out to the hall. She could not see the sudden slump of Duncan's broad shoulders as he watched her small, dignified figure disappearing through the door into the master bedroom.

The next two weeks passed in a blur of meaningless days and sleepless nights for Noramary. Day after day she searched her mind and heart, trying to discover the key that would unlock the source of Duncan's blind rage.

Janet's words came back to Noramary tauntingly. Her description of her brother's "ruthless unforgiveness when betrayed" took on new meaning. If Duncan, for whatever reason, thought she had betrayed him, how could they ever be reconciled?

A pervasive gloom hung over Montclair, diminishing the cheerfulness Noramary's endearing personality had brought to the household. The servants seemed to feel it, too, and went about their daily work as if on tiptoe. Ellen, from whom Noramary found it difficult to conceal anything, observed her mistress with characteristic sharpness, and set her mouth in a tight line as Noramary's growing unhappiness became more apparent. But Noramary, unable to explain to herself what had happened, could confide in no one.

Feeling lonely and abandoned, Noramary threw herself on her only hope, her faith that God had brought her to Montclair for His purposes and, no matter how it might appear, would continue to uphold her if she trusted Him. Even as she wept, on her knees, face buried in hands, she told herself He was always true to His Word, and clung desperately to the Scripture promise: "I will never fail thee nor forsake thee." It was her lifeline, that thin thread holding her back from the brink of despair.

November, with its bleak, gray days, brought with it a dreary sameness that Noramary found almost unbearable. The strain of the estrangement imposed by Duncan was gradually wearing her down.

Then something happened to break the awful monotony of Noramary's days and shed a ray of light on the darkness that had threatened to engulf her. An invitation to the annual pre-Christmas party came from Cameron Hall. Noramary received it with delight. But if she had entertained any hopes that the prospect of a social outing at Cameron Hall would soften Duncan's attitude or thaw his unremitting coldness toward her, they were dashed at once by his indifferent comment.

"Well, I suppose we have to go," he said with a shrug. "We can't offend my best friends, but I have no taste for it." And he turned away.

In spite of her disappointment at Duncan's reaction, Noramary continued to hope that once in the festive atmosphere at Cameron Hall, seeing friends and neighbors alive with the holiday spirit, Duncan might realize the pointlessness in maintaining his stubborn silence. How could anything breach the rift that daily widened between them unless he told her the source of it?

All she could do was try, Noramary decided. She would look her best and pray that the affection he had once felt for her might be revived. That as Scripture exhorted, "a wife's sweet spirit" might win over her husband.

And, on the night of the Camerons' party, if Noramary were to believe the adoring Delva, she did indeed look her loveliest. The dress she was wearing was not one of Winnie's cast-offs, but had been a gift from Aunt Betsy. Cut from a length of crimson velvet, its low, square neckline was edged with lace stiffened with gilt; the underskirt and draped paniers, of brocaded satin.

"Jes' waits 'til the Marster sees you!" declared Delva. "He'll be that proud!"

If only . . . thought Noramary wistfully.

Just as she was putting the finishing touches on her hair, there was a tap on the door from Duncan's dressing room. Surprised, Noramary turned from her mirror expectantly. He had not entered the bedroom for all these weeks.

Noramary held her breath as Duncan, looking handsome in a dark broadcloth coat, buff knee britches, and ruffled shirt, stepped in. He brought from behind his back the jewel case Noramary recognized as containing the Montrose rubies. She had not worn them since the night of Janet's farewell party.

Perhaps this was a gesture on Duncan's part to bridge the chasm of their estrangement. Her heart fluttered hopefully. But one look at his stony countenance killed that foolish notion.

"For you to wear tonight," he said brusquely. "The rubies."

"Oh, I was not sure you'd want me to wear them," she said in a low, controlled voice. She had left off the betrothal ring in the past weeks, feeling it was a farce. She now felt the same about the rubies.

"It is simply that people will expect to see them tonight," he said and paused. "As soon as you're ready, we can leave," he called over his shoulder as he turned away.

Wordlessly Noramary watched him walk back into

his dressing room. She quickly gathered her injured pride around her like a ragged shawl. Feeling Delva's eyes upon her, she gave no hint of her grief. It wouldn't do to give the servants more to gossip about.

With trembling hands, Noramary fastened the brooch to the shoulder of her gown, then slipped the earrings into her earlobes. The deep color of the jewels, caught in the light from the candles on Noramary's dressing table, shimmered like claret wine in crystal, she thought. Then the random thought flashed into her mind . . . more like heart's blood. For her own heart seemed to be bleeding inside her. Would Duncan never speak to her with tenderness nor look at her with love again? It seemed a cruel reality.

Noramary mounted the steps eagerly, grateful that their silent ride in the forced intimacy of the carriage, was over.

Jacqueline greeted her affectionately, exclaiming over her, complimenting her costume. Then she looked up at Duncan and shook her finger in mock reproach.

"Shame on you, Duncan, for not bringing Noramary over to visit us more often! Do you keep her prisoner at Montclair, for your pleasure alone?"

Duncan looked uncomfortable, but Jacqueline never noticed. She was far too busy signaling one of the maids to take their cloaks. Then, slipping her arm companionably through Noramary's, she insisted on taking her around personally to meet the other guests.

The house was beautifully decorated for the occasion. Garlands of galax leaves were wound between the banisters of the curved center staircase, crimson ribbons tied at the posts. Vases of nandina, cedar and pittosporum, and shiny holly boughs bright with berries, adorned every table. On the mantelpiece were vivid arrangements of pine cones, evergreens and candles, and in the dining room, where candles shone in crystal-prismed holders, a wreath of fruit, bayberry, nuts and cones centered the polished mahogany table set for sixteen.

For all the gaiety that surrounded her, Noramary found herself hard put to keep a smiling face. All her anticipation of this evening, her hopeful expectation that it might be a turning point in her relationship with Duncan faded in the face of his indifference. He kept his distance from her and spent the entire evening talking with others, ignoring her completely.

When dinner was served, Noramary found herself seated at James Cameron's right, with Duncan far down the table beside Jacqueline. The table was laden with a bountiful meal, the dishes having been concocted from food grown in the plantation's gardens and orchards. Noramary, distracted as she was, could only pick at the succulent food before her, though she tried to taste everything so as not to cause her host embarrassment.

For Noramary, the evening lengthened interminably as an endless round of toasts began. It seemed each gentlemen felt constrained to offer a toast, not only to the ladies present, but to each couple as well. Noramary's apprehension mounted as Duncan's turn approached, though it was James Cameron whose toast she dreaded most.

James had been flatteringly attentive throughout the dinner hour, telling Noramary what a blessing she was to Duncan, how happy his friends were that his lonely bachelorhood was ended, that he had taken to wife such a beautiful bride. As he got to his feet to propose the next toast, Noramary felt herself go rigid.

"My dear and honored guests—I want to propose a toast to a special man, one whom I regard as my closest friend and neighbor," he began, raising his glass. "Duncan Montrose, of Montclair.

"Montclair has always been esteemed for its splendid crops, its fine horses, its excellent hospitality—" He paused as the chorus of "Hear! Hear!" swelled among the guests and the tinkling of silver being gently tapped against the wine goblets; then continued— "From now on it should be known for its beautiful mistress as well. . . . To Noramary!" The gentlemen rose to their feet as if one, lifting their glasses to her, and a murmur of approval circled the table. She colored prettily, wishing nothing so much as that this evening would be over.

But the judge was not finished. He turned in Duncan's direction and bowed slightly. "My fervent wish is that, in the years to come, there will be many children to bless this charming couple and to fill their home with great joy."

Noramary's hand, holding a long-stemmed water goblet, began to tremble. His words seemed to halt all thought except her desire to know what Duncan must be thinking and feeling. She repressed the impulse to steal a quick glance to see how Duncan had reacted to the toast.

But she had no opportunity, for James was leaning toward her, diverting her attention, and in a stage-whisper, asked mischievously, "Can you guess what Jacqueline has planned for tonight's entertainment?"

Trying to appear interested, she listened politely. As a memento of the evening, each guest would carry home a profile of himself or herself, cut from black paper by a professional silhouettist. It was a skilled art, and the guests were delighted when the plan was announced.

"What fun!" exclaimed one of the ladies to Noramary. "I've always wanted to have my silhouette done. They're really quite an amazing likeness, I understand."

Noramary watched with fascination as the little man carefully surveyed his subject with narrowed, measuring eyes. Then, folding a sheet of black paper, he began to cut with sharp scissors, turning the paper carefully in his hands as he snipped. It was an astonishing thing to see.

Before she was quite prepared, it was Noramary's turn to sit for the artist. Because everyone gathered around the subject, watching the master silhouettist at work, she struggled to overcome her natural reluctance to be the center of attention, thinking that if the portrait turned out well, it would make a nice Christmas gift for her aunt and uncle.

She took her seat as instructed, her body turned so that a lighted candelabrum threw her profile sharply against the white wall of the paneled parlor wainscoting.

"Ah, what an enchanting profile!" said the artist, and for a few minutes there was absolute silence as he worked.

When he had finished, he held it up for Noramary to see, then quickly dabbed some mucilage from a small pot beside him and applied the silhouette to a stark white stiffened paper board. "Voilá!"

Jacqueline leaned over Noramary's shoulder to admire the artistry. "It's lovely, Noramary."

"I guess it is a surprising likeness. Perhaps I shall give it to my aunt and uncle for Christmas," she said.

"I notice you cut two at the same time, Monsieur Varny," Jacqueline remarked.

"Yes, it is my custom. Two thicknesses provide a firmer material with which to cut," he explained.

"May I have the extra one of my friend, then?" Jacqueline asked charmingly.

Shortly afterward, Duncan appeared. "It's time for us to go. I'll wait here while you get your cloak, then we'll say our good nights and be on our way."

The words were so terse, so unlike Duncan's former courteous consideration of her, that Noramary felt again the wound of their estrangement. But she went to get her cloak and muff, pausing only long enough to gain her composure before returning to the drawing room.

At least she had something to look forward to,

something pleasant to occupy her thoughts on the ride home, she reminded herself: She and Duncan would be going to Williamsburg for the holidays. He had promised Aunt Betsy. Surely he would keep his promise.

CHAPTER 17

SINCE IT WAS A CHRISTMAS DAY TRADITION at Montclair for the master to distribute gifts—bolts of bright calico, indigo cloth, new hats and scarves, jugs of molasses, flour and candy—to the servants, Noramary and Duncan had not left for Williamsburg until the following day.

The entourage had left Montclair before daybreak, and even though the country roads were rutted by winter rains and hardened by freezing weather, they had made good time.

There was the hint of snow in the crisp air of the December dusk when their carriage rumbled through the streets of Williamsburg, and Noramary's heart lifted with anticipation.

As the coachman slowed the horses to a more sedate pace through the residential part of town, Noramary felt a surge of nostalgia at the sight of the lighted candles in the windows. Here, at least, things were as they had always been. Families gathering to share the happy season, carolers raising familiar hymns at each door, party-goers on their way to holiday festivities. At Christmas, Williamsburg was at its best.

When they passed a house marked by a wooden sign at the gatepost: HUGH STEDD, PHYSICIAN, Noramary's heart twinged sharply. The familiar figure of Robert's uncle emerging from the front door brought a rush of memories—memories too dear, too sweet not to recall.

Noramary had locked away thoughts of Robert as the bittersweet keepsakes of a love best forgotten, but recently, in her loneliness, she found herself thinking of the past, of Robert, of the innocent love they had shared.

As they drew up in front of the Barnwells', Noramary was already on the edge of her seat, ready to alight as soon as the carriage door swung open. But Duncan put out a restraining hand, enclosing her wrist in a hard grasp, and said in a voice intense with warning, "I hope I do not need to remind you that our private difficulties should remain just that. I don't know how much of a confidante either your aunt or your cousins are to you; however, I do not wish to have our problems discussed with anyone. Is that understood?"

Stricken by the harshness of his admonition, Noramary was momentarily speechless. By the time she could respond, her voice was shaky.

"I understand *what* you are saying, Duncan, even though I still do not understand *why!* Whatever has made you so angry with me?" She shook her head as if to clear it. "Duncan, it's Christmas, a time for forgiveness, for joy, for love. In the spirit of this blessed season let us forgive one another, let us love . . ."

His grip only tightened on her arm. This time he spoke through clenched teeth, his tone gritty with irony.

"Must I repeat myself, Noramary? Can you not

understand that to all *appearances* we are a happily married couple, home for the holidays?"

Noramary closed her eyes for a second, then opened them and looked at Duncan with sorrow. "Yes, Duncan, I do understand," she said wearily.

She did not have time to say anything more, for at that moment the carriage door was opened, and at the same time the Barnwells' door flung wide, enveloping them both in the cheery glow from the house. She heard the excited welcoming cries of Sara and Susann as they bounded down the steps for a hug, followed quickly by Laura, then Aunt Betsy and Uncle Will's glad greetings. All this should have swept Noramary up in comforting warmth. Instead, she felt numbed by Duncan's icy indifference.

But there was more for Noramary to endure, to accept with a bravado she could not feel. Over the clamor and chatter of her little cousins' welcome, Duncan's words to her aunt and uncle fell like stunning blows.

"I shall be staying at our townhouse while we're in Williamsburg," he was saying. "I have some pressing business to attend to while I'm here—lawyers to consult about some recent land acquisitions and . . . some other matters. My hours will be erratic. I felt it would be best to spare your household this inconvenience, Aunt Betsy."

This, then, was Duncan's solution to the problem of sharing a room with her! Noramary realized, with a sinking heart, that there would be no reconciliation during this festive holiday, after all.

Though she was not sure her aunt and uncle believed Duncan's explanation, they accepted it graciously. So, as Duncan had requested, Noramary played her role of a wife home for a visit, hiding her secret sorrow under a smile and a cheerful countenance.

On New Year's Eve, as was their custom, the entire Barnwell family attended the early evening church service. Sitting beside Duncan in the family pew, Noramary was overcome with sadness. In this church . . . at that very altar . . . they had pledged their hearts and lives "from this day forward" in the sight of God and the gathered company of friends and loved ones.

There had been a promise of love in Duncan's eyes then, Noramary remembered, where now there was veiled contempt, almost as if he could not bear the sight of her. He stood a breath away from her as they rose to sing the opening hymn, but he might as well have been a thousand miles distant.

Noramary tried to control the urge to weep by focusing on the beautifully decorated interior. This little church, so like the small stone chapel near Monksmoor Priory, meant so much to her. In that other time and place, Nanny Oates had taken her as a very little girl to morning services, vespers, evensong.

Upon arriving in Virginia, suddenly surrounded by everything unfamiliar, Noramary had found a sense of identification in the recognizable ritual, the scent of candles, the old songs. It was here, when all else was confusion and frightening, that Noramary had found that comfort and true peace "that passeth understanding."

As the service proceeded, Noramary realized how much she had missed going to church regularly since moving to the country. Now when she needed it most, she had been deprived of this kind of strengthening help.

The music seemed particularly melodious and inspiring, the sermon appropriate and thoughtful. Yet, because of her inner turmoil, Noramary felt bereft. Her mind wandered and all she could seem to relate to was one brave, sputtering candle among all the other steadily burning candles, struggling not to go out. *Like me*, she thought, her throat aching with unshed tears, *just trying to survive!*

Duncan had said they must return to Montclair on New Year's Day, explaining to the Barnwells that duties awaited him at the plantation. But there would be one last event before they left—a New Year's Eve party at the Langley home.

Noramary had brought the crimson velvet dress she had worn to the Camerons' Christmas party, and some of the old excitement returned as she dressed for the evening. She took great pains with her hair and, at Laura's suggestion, wore it piled high, with curls falling behind each ear.

When she fastened in the ruby earrings Duncan insisted she bring to Williamsburg, Laura gasped, "My goodness, Noramary! I never saw such jewels! They are magnificent!"

"The Montrose Bridal Set," she explained in a toneless voice. "It's traditional for Montrose wives to wear them on special occasions."

Laura touched the brooch with a tentative finger. "Diamonds and rubies . . . they must be priceless!"

Noramary gave a short, mirthless laugh. "Like the valiant wife?"

Laura looked blank.

Noramary shook a playful finger at her cousin. "Don't tell me you've forgotten all the Proverbs we had to memorize! Remember 31:10? 'Who shall find a valiant wife, for her price is above rubies'?"

"And so you are!" responded Laura loyally. "Duncan must know how fortunate he is. Well, they're gorgeous and will look perfect with your gown. Don't keep him waiting too much longer!" And blowing Noramary a kiss, she skipped gaily out of the room.

When Noramary came downstairs moments later she found Duncan, looking splendid in a royal-blue jacket, black breeches, white ruffles at throat and wrist, waiting for her. Uncle Will was also in the hall.

"How lovely you look, my dear!" declared her uncle. "Duncan should be the proudest gentleman in all of Williamsburg tonight, escorting such a beauty."

She darted a quick glance at Duncan, who made no comment at all, although his eyes swept her from the top of her head to the tips of her tiny, satin-shod feet.

A short coach ride later, they arrived at the Langleys' doorstep, where the sound of spritely music and light-hearted laughter floated out into the crisp December night air.

In the entry hall one of the scarlet-coated servants helped them off with their wraps. Noramary felt her heart lift as she and Laura, like two moths drawn to a flame, followed the flow of music to the doorway of the ballroom.

Tapping her foot to the lively lilt of the music, Noramary was intent on watching the musicians perform when suddenly Laura clutched her arm and said under her breath, "Why, there's *Robert Stedd*! I didn't know he and his uncle had returned. They've been in England and Scotland since last fall. Robert is to attend medical school in Edinburgh, I understand."

Noramary felt as if she had turned to stone. All the noise of merriment, the shimmering candlelight, the music and dancers all seemed to dissolve, leaving her alone with only the echo of her heart's wild beating.

Robert! The possibility of running into Robert here at the Langleys' party had not even occurred to her. She vaguely remembered Aunt Betsy's mentioning, in one of her letters, the fact that he and his uncle had gone to England. But since then, her own life and its unexpected complications had occupied her attention.

Suddenly Noramary was aware of Duncan standing directly behind her and, at the same time, of Robert catching sight of her as he turned to speak to a friend.

The orchestra started up again, this time for the Roger de Coverly, the riotous reel Virginia had adapted for itself from the more sedate English version of the dance.

"Would you do me the honor, ma'am?" she heard Duncan ask Aunt Betsy.

"With the greatest pleasure!" replied her aunt, who still liked to dance.

Noramary frozen in uncertainty, saw Duncan lead her aunt onto the floor. Laura was quickly claimed by a partner, and Noramary found herself standing alone, riveted by Robert's intense gaze. And now he was making his way toward her.

He moved with the same easy grace she remembered, but in his stylish English-tailored clothes, he had lost his boyish look. His expression was serious as he approached. No smile softened the gravity of his mouth. Only his eyes spoke volumes as he came closer. Then he was standing in front of her and, with a kind of ache that bruised Noramary's tender heart, she realized Robert looked older. But then she was older, too. It was a long time ago since last spring when they had both been very young.

Frantically Noramary's eyes darted around the room, seeking an escape. But before she could flee, Robert was speaking her name softly, fervently.

"Noramary . . . what unbelievable luck to find you here."

All the old emotions rushed up in Noramary. All the memories merged into a dizzying blur. All the happy times they had known together as beloved companions—sharing, laughing, teasing, confiding, dreaming, planning, the hidden notes, the secret meetings. It had all been so innocent, so carefree, so loving.

Feeling that many eyes must be observing this reunion, Noramary's breath came shallowly as she held out her hand to him. Robert took it, raised it to his lips.

"Robert, how well you look," Noramary murmured, knowing how inane the words must sound.

"And you, Noramary, are more beautiful than ever." Robert raised an eyebrow. That gesture left much unsaid, but his insinuation was clear to her.

"I would ask you to dance, but I'd rather talk. Could we find some quiet place . . . just for a few minutes?" he asked, his eyes never leaving her face.

She found his intensity disturbing. "I think it better if we converse here," she replied formally, although her heart was pounding.

The music, enhanced by the sound of the dancers' feet, suddenly seemed louder. His fingers still held her hand and she felt an increased pressure.

"Surely two old friends can slip away to find a peaceful corner to renew acquaintance. . . . I don't think anyone would find that unseemly," he persisted Then, with more gravity, "Noramary, I must talk to you . . . alone. Is that too much to ask after all these months?"

"Robert, I am a married lady now. I cannot leave the dance with you. The gossips would have a field day!"

"In this merry crowd, filled with holiday cheer and punch as well? Come, Noramary, we'll dance this one minuet together, if that will satisfy your sudden penchant for propriety . . . then we'll find a convenient doorway and. . . ."

Before Noramary could protest further, Robert took her hand and led her out onto the dance floor. The slow, measured precision of the minuet allowed for ample opportunity to look into her partner's eyes, and Noramary found it difficult to avoid his magnetic gaze. They followed the dance to its finale, when each couple in turn bent low to sweep through the arch formed by the clasped hands and uplifted arms of the other dancers. With a skillful maneuver, instead of escorting Noramary around to the other end of the line to form another link, Robert whisked her off the floor and out into the hallway.

Never relaxing his firm grip on her elbow, Robert rushed her down the corridor and into one of the small rooms opening off the center hall. As if in a dance step, he whirled her through the door and spun her around, then closed the door behind them.

The minute she heard its click behind them, Noramary knew the folly of Robert's ploy. Although in the society of the day, light flirtations were regarded with amusement, in her heart Noramary knew this was different. She and Robert had meant too much to each other to render meaningless any such meeting. Not only that, but her sacred vows, taken with Duncan at the altar, came back to her now with renewed significance.

In a torrent of pent-up emotion, Robert burst forth: "Forgive me, Noramary! I had to do this. It was all I could do not to take you in my arms the minute I saw you!" She took a step backward, but he continued. "I've missed you terribly, Noramary. Did you ever think of me, knowing how much I loved you, how I was missing you all these months? I didn't realize how much until tonight, when I turned and saw you coming through the door."

"Robert . . . please! What if someone saw us coming in here together? Can you imagine what a scandal . . ." She looked around the room for another exit. But there was only one door and Robert was leaning against it, barring the way. "Robert, how did you know I'd be here?"

"I *didn't* know, Noramary. I haven't had much stomach for social life . . . not since . . . not for some time . . . And now that I've been back with Uncle, I've been helping him in his practice. I wouldn't have come tonight except for the Langleys. Please, relax. There's no harm in a quiet chat."

Noramary's agitation eased somewhat with Robert's calm reassurance, and she took a moment to catch her breath. *This must be the Langleys' music room*, she thought, noting the harp standing in one corner. Like the rest of the house, this room was decorated for the holidays, with wreaths at the windows, garlands and candles on the mantelpiece, and the traditional Christmas kissing-ball—a beribboned, clove-studded orange—hanging from the brass chandelier in the center of the ceiling.

Both she and Robert saw it at the same time. Noramary stepped away, blushing furiously. But Robert gave a low chuckle and moved toward her, grabbing both her hands before she could put them behind her back.

"Ah, Noramary, you didn't used to be so shy. It's only a holiday custom. Come, for old times' sake," he said, the old teasing quality in his voice melting her resolve a little. "It's little enough between two dear friends. 'Dare I not ask a kiss nor beg a smile'?" he quoted pensively.

And with a sharp tug of nostalgia, Noramary remembered how Robert had often read poetry to her. His eyes held such an irresistible plea, such pain, that she was overwhelmed by a longing to comfort him and experience for herself that old affection, that nonjudgmental, unconditional love only Robert had ever given her.

What harm could one kiss do? she thought, as she took a step toward him and lifted her face, intending to press her lips against his cheek, but Robert encircled her waist with his hands and drew her to him.

Suddenly the door burst open, followed by a peal of laughter. Noramary and Robert jumped, startled, and turned to see another young couple at the door, evidently seeking a little privacy themselves. Their shocked expressions at finding the room occupied might have provided a shared moment of hilarity had not Aunt Betsy and Duncan been passing in the hallway at that precise moment.

141

Turning to see what the commotion was all about, the two standing in the hallway saw Noramary and Robert in the incriminating embrace. To her horror, Noramary realized it must appear as though they had been surprised in a lover's rendezvous.

Aunt Betsy was the first to recover and, always the arbiter, bustled forward, saying as if nothing were amiss, "Oh, there you are! I thought you two would be off somewhere reminiscing over old childhood mischief." She shook her finger at Robert. "You were always the naughty one, Robert, teasing Noramary and tricking her into leaving her chores so she could run off and play." She laughed merrily and, turning to Duncan, put her hand on his arm. "What a time I had with these two children, Duncan. And now here's Robert all grown up and almost a full-fledged doctor." She prattled on while the three other people in the little scenario stared at each other, speechless.

Then Aunt Betsy stopped her chatter and asked in all innocence, "But, Robert, I don't believe you've ever met Noramary's husband, have you, dear boy? And Duncan, this is the nephew of one of our oldest friends, Robert Stedd."

At the introduction a dark flush spread rapidly over Duncan's face, and a muscle tensed in his jaw.

"*Robert?*" he repeated. "Robert Stedd?" There was a steely quality in his voice as he repeated the name.

"Your servant, sir." Robert acknowledged, bowing slightly.

Noramary looked from one to the other as the two men evaluated each other icily. A tangible tension crackled between them. It was as if they recognized each other as adversaries—*rivals*—she thought, puzzled. For under the veneer of polite exchanges seethed the truth that she belonged to Duncan in name; to Robert, by virtue of his steadfast love for her.

Finally Aunt Betsy broke the dreadful silence. Moving over to Robert, she slipped her hand through his arm. "Now, Robert, I do want to hear all about your plans to study in Scotland. Your uncle was just telling me and Will . . ." She steered him tactfully to the door, calling back over her shoulder to Noramary and Duncan, "Come along, you two. Supper will be served soon."

Duncan gave Noramary a stiff little bow, and offered her his arm without a word.

Noramary moved distractedly through the remainder of the evening. All she could think was how the scene he had happened upon must have looked to Duncan. Surely now, it would be futile to hope that he would ever understand the circumstances.

Outside, church bells began to chime the hour of midnight; inside, the wooden clackers, whistles and horns given to the party guests began an ear-splitting cacaphony, welcoming in the new year.

But Noramary's heart knew no joy. How could she join in the riotous celebration? For her, the year ahead held only the promise of bitterness and pain.

CHAPTER 18

NEW YEAR'S DAY DAWNED dreary and bleak. Noramary stared out the window of her bedroom at the
Barnwell home, sipping her morning tea and reliving
the events of the days just past. Parting with the
Barnwells would be difficult enough, knowing the
loneliness that awaited her at Montclair, but the long
ride from Williamsburg with the grimly silent Duncan
would be almost unbearable.

He had not spoken an unnecessary word to her
since leaving the Langleys' party the night before,
following the unfortunate incident of coming upon her
with Robert in what she felt sure he had mistaken as a
romantic rendezvous.

Even more than that, a note that had been delivered
to her that morning weighed heavily on Noramary's
heart. Essie, the upstairs maid, had brought it to her
with her breakfast tray that morning.

"A little boy who b'long to Dr. Stedd brang this
earlier, Miss Noramary. Say I was only to gib it to yo'
when you wuz by yo'self."

Noramary recognized Robert's handwriting even

144

before she tore open the envelope. The first few lines set her heart beating, flooded her face with color.

My darling Noramary,

What bittersweet joy to see you last night, and what sadness overcame me at so brief a meeting, and so soon a parting. Are you happy, my dearest? If only I knew that you were, *without any doubt*, without any uncertainty, then perhaps I could reconcile myself to having lost you. If that were a certain fact, I could then . . . somehow . . . go on with my life, assured that the one I care most for in this world was happy. Because I do not know if this is true, I have to live without that knowledge, and without you. The world indeed looks gray and without hope or cheer, and sometimes even without purpose. I will always hold you in my heart, since I cannot and never again will hold you to my heart. I pray you are happy, that God will bless you richly.

Forever . . . your most affectionate,

Robert

Noramary glanced out the window. The day was gray, heavy with snow clouds rolling across the wintry sky. A blustery wind whipped the branches of the bare trees, and Noramary shivered. Before she could sort her confused thoughts, a little tap at the door was followed immediately by Aunt Betsy's rosy face.

"Are you almost ready, dear? Duncan has arrived and is anxious to get underway before the weather worsens. Do you need any help with packing?"

Guiltily Noramary started, as if her aunt could possibly read her mind. Rising, she tucked Robert's note surreptitiously in the jewel case lying open on the dressing table. Then she snapped the lid shut and turned quickly to answer her aunt's inquiry.

"No thank you, Aunt Betsy. And, yes, I'm nearly ready."

Her heart was pounding crazily, and she wondered if the expression on her face in any way betrayed her state of mind. Nothing much had ever escaped her aunt's keen observation.

Noramary folded a chemise and placed it inside a small portmanteau she had been packing. Then she stood for a moment, distracted, trying to compose herself.

"I suggest you hurry, dear. Duncan is not a patient man," Aunt Betsy reminded her gently.

There seemed to be some special significance in that remark, Noramary thought, glancing at her aunt. And indeed there was, as Aunt Betsy's next words confirmed.

"My dear Noramary, it pains me to speak of this, but I feel I must. It was foolish and indiscreet of you and Robert to go off by yourselves as you did last night. I know neither of you considered the possible scandal such action might bring, but surely you remember your upbringing—the things your Uncle Will and I have tried to teach you. Christian ladies should not give even the slightest appearance of wrongdoing."

Noramary felt the sting of tears. To be so rebuked by her aunt cut her to the quick. There was no need to try to explain. She knew she stood accused of, if not deliberate flaunting of convention, certainly at the very least, irresponsible behavior. Such indiscretion was inexcusable, she knew.

There was another knock at the door. This time it had a peremptory sound and, when Aunt Betsy opened it, Duncan stepped into the room.

"We must leave at once, Noramary, if we are to avoid getting caught in a snowstorm," he said curtly. "Are you ready?"

Noramary quickly closed her portmanteau.

"You forget your jewel case," Aunt Betsy reminded her.

Remembering Robert's note hidden inside, Noramary's heart nearly stopped. She started to reopen the latches of her luggage when Duncan moved quickly to the dressing table and picked up the velvet box. "I'll take it."

146

Noramary felt as though she would faint. She knew Duncan kept the Montrose Bridal Set, along with other valuables, locked away in a strongbox in the library at Montclair. There was little chance he would open it before putting it away . . . but how could she retrieve Robert's letter? What if Duncan found it?

Sick with apprehension, there was nothing Noramary could do but watch helplessly as Duncan slipped the narrow case into the inside pocket of his coat.

"Ready?" he asked her, holding out her cape.

Noramary allowed him to place the jade green wool cape around her shoulders. With hands that shook she fastened the braid frogs, then reached for a beaver muff and slipped her suddenly clammy hands inside. Silently she passed through the door he held open for her, preceded by her aunt.

Feeling dizzy, Noramary endured the farewells at the bottom of the stairs, then, on Duncan's arm, went out to the waiting carriage.

On the long journey to Montclair, Noramary huddled in one corner, pretending to sleep. Her mind, however, was racing. Every once in a while she glanced over at Duncan, who was staring out the carriage window, lost in his own dark thoughts.

Besides the pressing problem of recovering Robert's incriminating note, how, she asked herself, was she to endure this loveless marriage, this cold indifference?

It was late when they finally reached Montclair, barely ahead of the first real winter storm, and Noramary awoke at dawn to a world blanketed in snowdrifts.

She had slept only fitfully and, during the night, startled into wakefulness by nightmares, had lain staring into the darkness. Her every thought, waking or sleeping, was of Duncan and what might happen if he opened the jewel case and found Robert's note.

Housebound by the blizzard for the next week,

Noramary lived in an agony of fear, praying constantly for God's mercy—and for Duncan's.

At the beginning of the third week in January the snow began to melt, making the roads passable once more. With the moderating temperatures came a message from Jacqueline Cameron that offered Noramary a change from her prison of doubt and fear. It was an invitation to visit Cameron Hall.

"It will be a ladies house party," wrote Jacqueline in her flowing script, "although husbands are welcome! The fashion dolls I ordered from Paris have arrived, and I thought you would enjoy seeing the latest Parisian styles."

For ladies in the Virginia colonies, the arrival of the so-called "fashion dolls," actually small manikins dressed in the height of fashion, was always a high point of the year. From these tiny models wearing miniature clothing, they could view the latest in fashionable attire, cut patterns from them, and have them copied by skilled seamstresses. Noramary remembered how Aunt Betsy had always anticipated the twice-yearly event in Williamsburg.

After receiving the invitation, Noramary's initial enthusiasm waned as she wondered what Duncan's reaction would be. Would he allow her to make such a visit? Would he allow her to go?

She gathered her courage and went to find him. He was in the library, sitting at his desk with a sheaf of papers in his hand. At her entrance Duncan looked up with a frown. Few words had passed between them since their return from the holidays. Noramary knew the incident with Robert Stedd had not been forgotten. This, compounded by whatever else had embittered him, made the wall between Noramary and Duncan even more impenetrable.

When she mentioned Jacqueline's invitation, his only reaction was to inquire when she would be leaving.

"Jacqueline says she will send her carriage for me tomorrow afternoon, if I can go. Her man, Micah, is waiting in the servants' quarters to take my answer back to her."

"Then by all means, do as you wish," Duncan said indifferently.

"Thank you, Duncan," she said in a small voice. Then she stood there, twisting her hands nervously while she pondered the advisability of making another request.

"Yes? Is there something more?" he asked in an annoyed tone of voice.

"Well . . . I was wondering, Duncan. Since there will be a festive party . . . might I wear the Bridal Set?" Noramary's heart was beating wildly. What if he had already checked the jewels and found Robert's note among them?

Duncan said nothing at first. Then, he pushed back his chair, stood, and went to the locked cabinet where he kept the strongbox.

Breathlessly Noramary watched as he unlocked it and withdrew the rectangular case. Her mouth went dry in terror.

Please, Lord, don't let him open it!

Duncan stood for what seemed an endless moment, simply holding the case thoughtfully. Then, without a word, he turned and handed it to her.

Noramary's legs managed to propel her through the study door and out into the hallway without giving way. But once she was safe in the haven of her bedroom, she fell to her knees beside the bed, unable to stem the torrent of tears. She opened the case with trembling hands. To her immense relief Robert's letter lay, undisturbed, on the top.

Noramary got up from her knees and, taking the letter, she hid it carefully under her lingerie in one of the dresser drawers. When she was calmer, when she could think exactly what to say, she would answer the letter, she told herself weakly.

149

Recalling the scene as she rode to Cameron Hall the next day, Noramary thought ruefully that it might have been better if Duncan had refused her request. At least that would have signaled his interest in whether she came or went. Even that small knowledge would have been some consolation.

Suddenly aware of her nagging headache, she pressed her fingers to her throbbing temples. If it had not been for her desperate need to escape the oppressive atmosphere at Montclair, she might not have made the effort to go. Lately Noramary had experienced some troubling physical disturbances to add to her emotional distress. Just this morning she had awakened with the dull headache and a general feeling of malaise, and only the prospect of Jacqueline's delightful company had prodded her to overcome her lethargy and follow through on her plans.

There had been no sign of Duncan upon her departure. It was not surprising. He had taken to riding out to the fields very early in the morning, not returning until late. Some days, when he was surveying a distant part of the plantation, she knew he stayed over at the cottage at night instead of returning to Montclair. But not giving her the courtesy of seeing her off before her week's absence was yet another rejection to be concealed beneath a bright smile when she arrived at Cameron Hall.

By the time her carriage drew up to the door, she had assumed her usual cheerful outlook, and no one, not even Jacqueline who knew her well, would have suspected the pain she harbored in her heart.

Noramary was greeted with great warmth by her hostess and introduced to the three other houseguests, ladies from neighboring plantations, all of whom she had met at the Christmas party. Each of them, liberated from the stultifying isolation of the long winter and icy roads that had kept them from the company of congenial friends, was eager to enjoy the pleasant interlude and the mood was soon one of frivolous gaiety.

The next two days at Cameron Hall were a delightful blend. The mornings were spent in examining the fashion dolls, making sketches of the various costumes, consulting each other about patterns, fabrics, and adaptions of the styles. After the midday meal, they retired for a long afternoon nap.

But it was the evenings, when they gathered in the drawing room for more conversation or music, that Noramary found most enjoyable. Here, amid friends and a relaxed atmosphere of cheerful repartee and laughter, Noramary thrived. Here, she did not have to watch her every word, fearful of saying or doing something that would bring a frown to Duncan's brow or a cool stare. For Noramary, it was a time of pleasant diversion—feeling amused and amusing and, above all, accepted. More than anything, she felt herself again after the dreary winter in Duncan's reluctant company.

On the last evening of her visit, Jacqueline came into the guestroom where Noramary was dressing for dinner.

"Ah, *cherie,* it has been such a pleasure to have you here these past days, but I have not had a moment for private conversation. I thought you looked a bit pale and peaked when you arrived, and the thought crossed my mind that perhaps . . . ? *Mais non,* I'm sure it is only my imagination, for you seem rosy and radiant now. You have enjoyed yourself here, *n'est ce pas?* "

"Oh, it's been wonderful, Jacqueline. I've had such a good time, I hate to . . ." Noramary checked her impulsive words before she admitted that she dreaded going home.

Jacqueline did not seem to notice, but continued smoothly, "But then, the handsome Duncan must be pining away for the return of his bride, *qui?* " Without waiting for a reply, she went on: "I shall never forget how excited Duncan was after you became engaged. How anxious he was that the house would be in perfect condition for your arrival, everything finished for you!

"You are a very lucky girl, Noramary, to catch such a man! You know half the mamas in the county were hoping to have him for a son-in-law!" Jacqueline laughed at Noramary's puzzled expression. "You didn't know that? Well, let me tell you. I can't count how many friends tried to select just the right bride for Duncan. All the daughters, nieces, sisters who have been trotted out for his approval! Ah, la! But let me tell you a secret—I never saw him so happy as when he rode over to tell us there had been a change of plans, that instead of the Barnwell girl, he was marrying her cousin. The look on his face, *cherie*! Oh, it was good to see! Duncan is a wonderful man . . . and I have seen many, but none better than he!"

Suddenly Noramary felt hot and sick and dizzy. Blood rushed into her face, then drained from her head as waves of nausea swept her. Jacqueline's face became a blur and the whole room tilted crazily. She tried to stand, but a smothering black mask came down upon her, choking off the air, and she slipped to the floor in a faint.

The next thing Noramary knew was the stringent aroma of smelling salts, the pressure of a cool cloth against the back of her neck, the support of gentle hands. As she regained complete consciousness, she saw that she was lying on the chaise lounge, with Jacqueline's anxious face hovering above her. Nearby stood a black maid, holding a cup of steaming fragrant tea.

"What happened?" Noramary asked weakly.

Jacqueline's worried pucker changed to a teasing smile. "But why didn't you tell us this happy news?

Or were you keeping it a secret for awhile? Do not worry, *cher* Noramary, soon you will feel better, you'll see. It is the first few weeks that are sometimes trying."

Noramary stared blankly at her hostess for a moment, bewildered. Then slowly, understanding came, followed immediately by dismay.

"Oh, no!" she covered her mouth with one hand. "I *can't* be! What will Duncan say?"

"What! Haven't you told him?" Jacqueline demanded in amazement. "But what *should* he say? "Duncan will be beside himself with joy, of course! Oh, yes!" she hastened on over Noramary's protest. "He adores you, and now even more, since you will bring him an heir to his vast lands and to his name!"

"But you don't understand!" Noramary shook her head forlornly, slow tears rolling unchecked down her cheeks.

"What is to understand? Duncan will be so happy at this news. Did you not see his reaction when my husband toasted him at the Christmas party? There is nothing Duncan wants more than many fine sons to follow him at Montclair."

Noramary continued shaking her head. But she knew she could not confide in Jacqueline what she did not know herself. Perhaps Duncan had once been happy to have her as his bride. Perhaps even once he had loved her. But now everything was different, everything was changed.

"You'll see, Noramary. What I'm saying is true. I only wish I could see Duncan's face when he hears his good fortune."

As she rode back to Montclair from Cameron Hall the next day, Noramary felt the news she carried to Duncan was more a burden than a blessing. She dreaded the moment when she would know his reaction, for of course he must be told.

It was Ellen rather than Duncan who greeted Noramary upon her return. The delay only fueled her apprehension. Perhaps it was for the best, she reassured herself. In the morning she would be more rested, better able to confront Duncan's anger or disdain, whichever it might be.

Still, as the hours passed, Noramary grew more and more distracted. When the strange weakness and nausea assailed her again, she went to lie down, telling Delva to tell her the minute Duncan came home.

She must have drifted off, for her bedroom was shadowed when she heard the dogs barking, always a signal of Duncan's homecoming, then the sound of his boots on the polished floor outside her room.

The door opened and he stepped inside.

"You wanted to see me?" he demanded. Approaching the bed, he frowned. "Your maid tells me you're feeling unwell. What is it?"

Noramary struggled to sit up. "Oh, it's nothing . . . really," she murmured hesitantly.

"It must be *something* . . . otherwise you wouldn't have asked to see me." His voice was stern. "Perhaps it is simply an attack of melancholy after your visit to Cameron Hall. Perhaps coming back to Montclair is the cause of your malaise. It is sad, but true, that life at Montclair can hardly rival that of either Williamsburg or Cameron Hall."

"Oh, no Duncan . . . it isn't that. Indeed, under the circumstances . . . my coming back to Montclair should be a time of *rejoicing*." Noramary forced herself to ignore his irony and to speak steadily and cheerfully. It was, she felt, a chance to right all the wrong between them, to end forever this state of bitter misunderstanding.

He turned to stare at her, bewilderment, doubt and uncertainty mingled in his expression.

Noramary took a deep breath and proceeded, "Duncan, we are to have a child."

The sudden silence that fell over the room was devastating in its totality.

Then Duncan spoke and his voice was edged with steel. "Correction, my dear!" Here he paused significantly. "*If* your condition is as you imply, it is *you* who are to have a child . . . not *we*. What kind of a fool do you and your close, loving, and oh-so-clever family take me for? First, they offer—as a 'substitute' to one flighty daughter—her more beautiful, brighter, more amiable, more charming cousin, as if she were some prize that I, the rejected suitor, should feel fortunate to win. Never a word that it would be convenient—nay, helpful, in fact—to get this lovely young woman off their hands before she did something indiscreet. . . . Or perhaps they were aware of other indiscretions that might have led to a less . . . shall we say . . . suitable marriage! At any rate, I admit I was taken in by this cleverly arranged substitution. More than that, I fell under the spell of this charming 'substitute bride.' Ah, yes, her demure, unassuming manner did quite beguile, and I fell prey to every well-planned move until—" He halted abruptly.

"So, Noramary, you find yourself with child. So be it. We are married. You bear my name. I should not disgrace either of us by disclaiming the child that you are carrying. But never . . ." and his voice deepened in cold intensity, "*never* insult me by insisting it is *mine*."

His words fell upon her like stinging blows.

"Duncan, you are wrong!" Noramary burst out. "Why can't you believe me? I have not . . . there has never been. . . ."

"Don't add to your shame with more lies. I have eyes! I saw you and Robert Stedd in Williamsburg. There was no mistaking the relationship between you. Nor did it escape my notice that you took the first opportunity to be alone with him, regardless of how it might look. . . . Please, spare me any more . . . spare us *both* more of these distressing scenes."

With that he spun on his heel and stalked out of the room, leaving Noramary quivering under the lash of his words.

CHAPTER 19

THE FIRST OF MARCH WAS BITTERLY COLD, ushering in a series of storms, each one worse than the one before. Rain, sleet and sudden snows followed one another in rapid succession.

Noramary, morning-sick as well as heart-sick, felt imprisoned and isolated. Duncan's unrelenting attitude numbed every emotion except the anguish of his constant rejection, the reason for which still remained a mystery to her.

What bothered her most was that there was no joy in the coming baby. The child of their supreme moment of love had found no welcome in the home he would inherit, none in his father's heart.

Because of the depressing sameness of her days, Noramary was tempted to daydreams of Williamsburg, of Robert, of what might have been. She prayed to be rid of them, for she knew they only added to her unhappiness and did nothing to give her hope of an eventual reconciliation with Duncan.

Seated at her escritoire at the window of the master bedroom one morning, Noramary tried once again to answer Robert's letter. She had taken it from its hiding place that morning and reread it through tear-blurred eyes. Poignant memories of all their happy times together now seemed so long ago. Another lifetime!

She took out stationery, dipped her quill into the inkwell and with pen poised to write, searched her mind for the words.

How could she answer truthfully Robert's question? Was she really happy? Anything she might say could give him false hope. To allow Robert to harbor hope was wrong. To let him linger in regret of what might have been was destructive. To prolong his yearning for her love was cruel. As long as he kept thoughts of her burning in his heart, he put his own soul in jeopardy. Didn't the Commandments themselves prohibit such thoughts? "Thou shalt not covet thy neighbor's wife." It was clear enough there. Even clearer in the New Testament. There was no other way than to write gently, firmly and finally to Robert, telling him he must forget her once and for all.

Determinedly she started to write, but each time she tried, the words sounded so stilted, so false, she scratched them out, crumpled up the paper, and started again. On about the fourth try she happened to look up from her desk and see Duncan ride by on his dapple gray horse.

With a heart sore with longing she watched them pass. The graceful beauty of the animal matched the proud bearing and set of the head of the rider. A powerful yearning wrenched Noramary, a desperate longing that the terrible misunderstanding could be solved, that they could know once more that soaring rapture. But it had been as brief as a candle flame, she thought sadly, and as quickly extinguished.

For a few minutes Noramary stared out the window. Although the severe winter storms had passed, the landscape was bleak. The rim of the mountains seemed like grim prison walls, locking her within this unhappy place.

As she looked a pale sun struggled through the pewter-colored clouds, and although a blustery wind was bending the bare tree branches, Noramary felt a sudden urge to go outside, get out of the house, out into the fresh air. A walk would do her good after the weeks she had been confined by the inclement weather.

She flung her cape around her shoulders, paused briefly to tell one of the servants she was leaving, and went outside. The wind whipped the folds of her cape like billowing sails, but the sharp bite of the wind felt invigorating.

Patches of snow still clung to the brown meadow, and icy drifts were piled under the low-hanging branches of the evergreens along the path to the woods. Noramary took long breaths and drew the crisp, exhilarating air deep into her lungs.

She walked along briskly, more conscious of her troubled thoughts than of the direction she was taking. When she found herself at the rustic bridge that curved over the creek that cut through the meadow, she stopped and paused to catch her breath. Inevitably she was reminded of that stormy night when this bridge had been washed away, forcing her to remain with Duncan in the little cottage overnight. That night when they had made those first, tentative moves toward understanding each other, getting to know each other. Everything had seemed possible then. Even learning to love each other.

The memory was bittersweet. Noramary stared hypnotically into the crystal clear water rushing over the stones, wishing she could somehow turn back the clock. Almost unconsciously, she continued on the path toward the cottage, as if following some inner leading. Soon she was on the little rise just above the hollow where the cottage nestled into the protective shelter of the trees. The next thing she knew, she was standing in front of the door. Moving as if in a dream long-remembered, or by the deep longing in her heart, she put her hand on the latch and lifted it. The door opened easily to her touch, and Noramary walked inside.

She went over to the fireplace, remembering the festive supper she and Duncan had shared in front of it. At least it had seemed so. She thought sadly of the strained dinners they now took together in the vast dining room at Montclair—each seated far apart at either end of the long table, with only a few words spoken in the presence of the servants waiting on them.

Ironically, she recalled how they had happily quoted the Psalmist over their meager supper that night. "Better a dry morsel with joy than a feast where strife dwells."

Noramary wandered about the little house, noticing the tasteful furnishings. Just as Cameron Hall bore the indelible stamp of its mistress's colorful personality, so this place where Duncan had lived for several years reflected his quiet dignity.

On the night of the storm, she had remained in the front room near the blazing warmth of the fireplace. The next morning she had gone into the bedroom only long enough to make a brief toilette. Now she moved through each room taking note of everything. It was a miniature of the great mansion down to the most minute detail. Everything was of the finest quality, the most precise craftsmanship. Duncan demanded perfection in everything.

There was also evidence of the more recent times when he had chosen to remain here rather than ride back to Montclair, the house where love had ceased to be, Noramary thought sorrowfully. A heavy, woolen outer jacket was hung carefully over a chair, a linen shirt discarded, a scarf flung onto the wooden settle.

160

Noramary stepped over to the door leading into the bedroom and pushed it open. As she might have expected of a man of Duncan's meticulous habits, the bedcovers were smooth, the quilt folded at the bottom of the four-poster bed. She was starting to leave when something caught her eye. Hanging over his graceful English desk in one corner of the room was her silhouette—the one cut by the artist at the Camerons' Christmas party!

Noramary went over for a closer look. There could be no mistake. It was the duplicate of the one she had given Aunt Betsy. But it was Jacqueline who had asked for the copy. Had she given it to Duncan? Or, and something like hope leaped in Noramary's heart, had Duncan asked for it?

If Duncan had come to despise her as much as it seemed, why would he want an image of her where he could see it often? It was a tantalizing question, one for which Noramary had no answer.

She sat down on the chair at the desk, staring at her silhouette, trying to make sense of this puzzling discovery.

How long she remained there, lost in thought, she never knew. But suddenly the rattle of rain against the window startled Noramary. Looking up, she noticed that the day had darkened considerably. She had come a long way from the main house. She must start back right away.

The wind had come up and she heard it keening down through the chimneys of the empty fireplaces and around the eaves. She stepped outside onto the porch. In the midst of these dense woods, it appeared as if evening had already descended. She pulled up the hood of her cape, drew its strings and tied them under her chin. The rain was spasmodic as she started out, but the wind was fierce and she bent her head against it and began to walk faster.

It seemed that she walked for some time at a brisk

pace when her legs began to tire. She stopped, arching her back and pressing with her fingers to relieve the ache. Looking around, she frowned. She should have come to the clearing that led into the meadow above Montclair by now, but she was still in thick woods.

Had she turned the wrong way when she left the cottage? Perhaps she had missed the path. She paused for a few minutes, trying to remember how she had come. Maybe it had been from the other direction. So she reversed her course. But this did not lead her to the opening she had hoped to find, either.

Feeling her legs quivering with exertion, she leaned against a tree to rest. By now the rain was threading through the trees, increasing steadily, so that soon the ground was soaked. In spite of her warm cape, Noramary, too, was drenched.

No matter, she would simply have to plow on. This must be the way back to Montclair, she told herself, stumbling forward again.

She couldn't have gone so far that it would be impossible to find her way back, she encouraged herself, though she had heard of people who traveled in circles through the wilderness, became lost, gave up in despair, and were eventually discovered only a few yards from their destination.

The rain turned to icy needles of sleet. Noramary ducked her head and forced herself on. Her thin slippers were already wet, and she was almost blinded by the freezing rain slicing in front of her and upon her, the wind slashing against her.

She bit her lip, trying not to cry out in fear and panic. Her feet slipped and slid on the now sodden ground. Once or twice she fell to her knees. She staggered up—her skirts, now heavy from the rain and mud, slowing her progress. The sleet had turned to snow. Driven by the mounting wind, the flakes struck her face in rapier-sharp particles. She stumbled on, stopping only to draw a ragged breath and rest, her hands clinging to the rough bark of the pine trees, fighting fatigue and a growing desperation.

It was then that she saw a light swinging in an arc, as though from a lantern. Breathless with hope, she watched as it grew brighter, stronger.

Then through the dark and the cold, she heard a familiar voice, rough with anxiety, calling . . . calling her name, hoarsely, over and over. . . .

"Noramary! Noramary . . . answer me!"

The light was a blinding square now directly in front of her. She held up one hand weakly and answered with utmost effort, "Here I am! Oh, Duncan, thank God!" before she felt her knees give way and she sank to the ground.

The next thing she knew, she was swung up in strong arms, the hood of her cape falling back, her wet hair streaming into her face.

She did not remember much about the jolting horseback ride in front of Duncan's saddle, his arms holding her tightly as he spurred his horse forward through the sheet of whirling snow.

She recalled being carried into the house, the circle of fearful dark faces around her, hearing Duncan's voice say harshly, "Ellen, get her out of these wet clothes and into a warm bed as fast as possible. She's soaked to the skin and already shaking with fever."

She roused herself enough to try to control her shivering and whisper guiltily, knowing she must have caused great concern and trouble by her absence in the storm, "I'm sorry. . . ."

"Never mind that, dearie." That was Ellen's voice with its soft Scottish burr. "We'll have you warm and cozy soon so's you won't catch your death of cold."

Noramary opened her large eyes, now unnaturally bright, and murmured, "It's nothing really . . . a slight chill."

Ellen gently helped her undress, while a frightened Delva was busily running the warming pan between

163

the sheets. Two other maids heated bricks in the fireplace, then wrapped them in thicknesses of flannel to place at her feet. Noramary alternately shivered and felt fiery hot, but protested that she would be fine in the morning. Soothingly, Ellen guided her over to the bed and, as tenderly as if she were a child, half lifted her aching body into bed.

Outside, the storm continued to rage, but no more so than did the fever in Noramary, who tossed and turned with troubled dreams. It was the same one she had had over and over in the past few months. She always seemed to be running, as if searching desperately for something or someone. There seemed to be a river rushing wildly between her and the object of her search. A mysterious figure stood on the other side, just out of reach, beyond the sound of her voice as she called his name. He never looked in her direction, and she would awake, sobbing and breathless.

Time after time, when she woke choking and hoarsely calling that name, Ellen was there. It was the same throughout the night—the fitful sleep, the dream, waking to Ellen's ministrations, then falling again into troubled sleep. Never once did she see the tall, shadowy figure standing just outside the half-open bedroom door.

The next few days were a blur to Noramary and were followed by weeks of slow recovery. She slipped in and out of consciousness as her fever mounted, aware only of the muted sound of movement around her; of hushed, yet urgent voices; of hands, blessedly cool on her burning skin; of a headache pounding so persistently that she could not think.

Then there was the night she awoke to an agonizing stab of blinding pain like the thrust of a sharp knife. She remembered crying out as a rushing shudder shook her frail body, and then she sank into oblivion. The pain was the last thing she remembered. It was days before Noramary was conscious of anything else.

Much later, she learned from Ellen the other part of the story: Of how, when she had not returned by dark, the frightened servants and a weeping Delva had gone to Ellen, who had sought Duncan in the plantation office. Hearing that their mistress had gone out early in the afternoon for a walk and had not yet returned, he had jumped to his feet.

"You are sure she didn't take her horse or get the small carriage from the stable, perhaps to ride over to Cameron Hall?" he demanded of the cluster of house servants and Ellen standing in a frozen line, awaiting the master's decision. They all shook their heads. "In that case, send word to the stables to saddle my horse, and get two of the men mounted to go with me. We must find her before it gets any darker or colder."

Noramary opened her eyes and turned her head slowly on the pillow to gaze out the window. Outside, the sky was blue and, on the branches of the trees, fragile green leaves shimmered in the sunlight. Somehow spring had come at last, she thought in surprise.

Vaguely she wondered what day it was, for she seemed to have lost all track of time. She tried to raise her head but felt rather light-headed and weak. Tentatively she moved, and in an instant Ellen's kind, worried face bent over her.

"You're awake, dearie. I'll get you some broth. The doctor said you must try to eat something soon. You've dwindled away to a mere nothing, you have."

"Ellen, what happened? I know I must have been ill, but I don't remember. . . ." Noramary's voice was faint.

For a moment Ellen's blue eyes misted with bright tears. "You've been *very* ill, dearie. We were that afraid that you might slip away altogether. But the Lord was good. Except, dearie. . . ." Ellen's hand covered Noramary's small, thin one with a sympathetic gesture. "You've lost the bairn. . . . The doctor said it was the high fever . . . it could not be helped. But you're not to be sad, dearie," Ellen continued briskly, plumping the pillows behind Noramary's head. "You weren't that far along, and he says there's plenty of time for babies!"

Part IV

"Hope deferred makes the heart sick, but when the desire comes, it is the tree of life."

Proverbs 13:12

CHAPTER 20

AUNT BETSY, ACCOMPANIED BY LAURA. arrived at Montclair in response to Duncan's urgent summons. She was shocked at the drastic change in Noramary's appearance. Her vibrant, glowing look was gone. Her skin, pale, almost transparent. Her slender body, wasted.

Within hours of her arrival, Aunt Betsy had come to the decision that Noramary must return with her to Williamsburg to be nursed back to health.

"I must say, Duncan, I am gravely concerned. To be very blunt, I fear for her life."

Duncan paled. "But the doctor has assured me Noramary is out of danger. . . ."

"That may be. However, the girl has suffered not only physically, but the other effects of losing her child may not yet be known. Unless we do something right away, Noramary might still slip away from us."

"Then, madam, I can only agree to whatever would be best for her," Duncan agreed.

"Right now she needs the bright company of her cousins and the activities of our busy household to distract her from her sorrow over the baby," Aunt Betsy continued firmly "Noramary is much too young to bear the natural depression she feels in this solitude. It will do her a world of good. Mark my words, we must all help her to get well, and we must begin now."

The decision was made and, while it was met with some reluctance and not a little resentment by Ellen who had nursed Noramary so faithfully, she relented when Duncan convinced her it was all for her beloved charge's good. Even Ellen could see that Noramary was getting no better, in fact, seemed to be losing ground each day.

Ellen helped bundle Noramary warmly into the carriage and, amid the flurry, the strangely formal farewell between husband and wife went unnoticed.

As they started down the drive from Montclair, Noramary turned and looked back through the oval window, and her heart was suddenly wrenched at the sight of the tall man standing on the porch. His shoulders were slumped in an uncharacteristic posture of dejection and defeat, and she thought of what Ellen had told her.

"He never left your bedside, ma'am, not for all those days you were sick. When I had to go take some slight repast or for some other necessity, or when he insisted I have a short nap, he would stay right there until I returned. Tender as a woman, he was! When you were out of your head, tossing and turning and calling out, he would soothe your head with cool cloths. He never seemed to tire. And when you lost the baby . . . why, I never saw a man so grieved!"

Grieved? Duncan, over a child he did not believe was his? Noramary could only shake her head in bewilderment.

For Noramary, the next few weeks passed in a peaceful montage of long, leisurely, sun-splashed days. She slipped back into the framework of life in the Barnwell house as easily as if she had never left, and the longer she stayed, the less real seemed her life at Montclair.

Spring had come to Williamsburg in a burst of delicate color of blossoming fruit trees and flowering bushes. The gardens of the town behind the neat boxwood hedges were rainbows of bright blooms. Noramary enjoyed sitting in the sunshine of the pleasant walled garden behind the Barnwells' home, in the lounge chair that had been placed there for her.

When she was relaxing there one day while Aunt Betsy filled her basket with mint leaves, Noramary sniffed the spicy fragrance appreciatively.

"You should plant an herb garden at Montclair, Noramary," Aunt Betsy remarked.

"Yes, I suppose I should," Noramary agreed passively,

Unknown to her, Aunt Betsy's words pierced Noramary's heart. With aching remembrance, she thought of that night at Montclair when she and Duncan had sat together at the window of their room, and he had asked her.

"What can I do to make you happy?"

"But you have already made me happy, Duncan."

"I want to do something special for you! Isn't there something you would like to have?"

"Well, "she had replied thoughtfully, "I would really like to have a garden."

"You shall have it, my darling!" he had declared emphatically, kissing her tenderly.

But there had been no garden. After that night there had only been a wasteland at Montclair.

Then one day the quiet stream of days was broken by two unexpected events.

Noramary was alone in the house one afternoon while Aunt Betsy and Laura were shopping. The little girls were in school; Uncle William, at his business office.

She had just come in from the garden and settled herself in the small parlor with some knitting when she had the sudden impression she was no longer alone. A shivery tremor tingled down her spine so positive was she that someone's gaze was upon her.

Lifting her head slowly, her eyes widened upon the figure standing in the doorway.

"Robert!" She dropped her knitting and gasped his name.

He came into the room and stood there gazing at her with a look of such longing that it touched the very depths of her heart. The bond of years embraced her in warmth, and she held out both hands in greeting. Remembering the carefree happiness they had known together, all her desolate loneliness faded, the weary emptiness of the past months fled.

For a few minutes her hands remained in his, and there were no words for all that was in each heart to say. Then Noramary, realizing the danger of this innocent meeting and what was in both their minds— the close companionship growing into innocent romance, the summer kisses, the impulsive promises— gently withdrew her hands. She needed to remind Robert—and herself—that everything was different now, everything changed.

"Sit down, Robert. I was about to have my tea and you must join me." Her voice trembled slightly.

"There's no need for that." He dismissed her suggestion with a gesture. "I came only because I heard you had been very ill, and I wanted to see for myself that you were all right."

Noramary reseated herself, picking up her knitting again. Perhaps the activity would still the shaking of her hands.

Robert stood by the fireplace, looking down at her. She felt uncomfortable under his close scrutiny, for one did not have to be a physician to see the changes wrought by her illness. Yet it was the more subtle changes carved into her face by her unhappiness that Robert noted. Her delicate-boned slenderness now verged on thinness, the rosy-cheeked roundness of her face had been replaced by a pale oval, the eyes that had once danced with mischief and fun were smoky blue pools of haunting sadness. Noramary knew he had not missed any detail.

She cast about for some topic to relieve the heavy silence that hung between them, but it was Robert who spoke first.

"I have been talking with your uncle, Noramary. He is writing some letters of introduction for me. I am leaving shortly to go to Scotland, where I will study for a year with a friend of my uncle's—a surgeon with an excellent reputation. He has been developing some new methods of surgery that I hope to learn so that when I come back . . ." His voice trailed away.

Noramary glanced up from her knitting to catch the look of grief in his eyes. She spoke quickly to mask the awful silence that was descending once more. "That sounds very interesting, Robert. I'm sure your studies will be most fascinating and . . ."

But Robert interrupted. "On, Noramary, surely we can talk of other things than my medical studies. There is so much I want to say, so much I need to know, so many unanswered questions. . . ."

"They are better neither asked nor answered, Robert," she said softly.

"Why cannot there be truth between us, Noramary?" Robert asked. "I realize you could not respond to the note I wrote you at Christmastime, but it would still mean so much to me to know . . . to be *sure* . . . that you are happy."

Noramary looked directly into Robert's earnest eyes, remembering with regret the day she had tried to write to him, the half-written letters she had left on her escritoire just before leaving for that ill-fated walk in the woods. She had gone to the cottage that day,

172

had found her silhouette over Duncan's desk. Then the storm had come and . . .

"Well, Noramary, are you? Have you been happy these months?" Robert's voice broke in upon her reverie.

She looked over at him. He was bending forward, his hands clasped on his knees, the clear, truth-seeking eyes searching her face.

Just then the door opened and Thomas, the Barnwell's butler, entered, bearing a silver tray. It took a few minutes for him to set it down and bring the serving table over in front of Noramary.

She willed her hand not to shake as she lifted the heavy silver teapot to pour the steaming tea into delicate cups. They were both silent until Thomas left the room, leaving the door discreetly open as befitted the situation of a married lady entertaining a gentleman.

But still Robert's question begged an answer.

Noramary's thoughts were in turmoil. She knew Robert deserved an answer. Yet how could she give him an answer that would satisfy him, yet remain loyal to her wifely vows to Duncan? To reveal the secret she had borne so long alone now seemed a betrayal.

In spite of everything that had happened, Noramary still believed her marriage vows were sacred. She recalled the words the minister had read from the book of Hosea on their wedding day.

I will betroth thee unto me *forever*,
Yes, I will betroth thee to me
In righteousness and justice
In lovingkindness and mercy.
I will betroth thee to me in *faithfulness*."

The words themselves, echoing in her mind, brought instant understanding of what she must do. Much as she loved Robert, would always love him, he was part of her past, her childhood, the other life she had put behind. That is where he belonged—in her past. She had to help him put *her* in *his* past, too. What they had once had together would never really end. It would be a lovely memory always. To try to make anything now of these chance meetings would only spoil those memories. He must understand that they both had to go on to other lives, other loves. Only if she freed him could Robert do that.

So when Noramary answered Robert, she spoke very gently but very positively. "Yes, Robert, I am happy." And by that affirmation she believed she was willing that happiness into existence.

With God's help I will find a way to be happy, she resolved, *and if not happy, then content.*

"Then I, too, am happy, Noramary," Robert said solemnly. He tried to smile. "I suppose there is nothing more to be said. I shall take my leave."

Noramary rose from her chair and, with a rustle of skirts, came around the tea table, holding out her hand to him. As she did so, her wide skirt brushed the knitting basket by her side, toppling it and spilling the contents onto the floor. A ball of yarn rolled toward Robert, stopping somewhere midway between them.

At the same time both Robert and Noramary moved to retrieve it, bending down simultaneously. Robert was quicker and collected the yarn ball, placing it in her cupped hand. Their fingers touched and, for a moment, all the old memories flowed back and, suspended in nostalgia, they stood looking into each other's eyes.

At that very moment a tall figure stepped into the doorway, blocking it and casting a long shadow into the sunny parlor. Startled, Noramary and Robert turned to see Duncan standing there, regarding them coldly.

"Duncan! What are you doing here? I didn't expect you!" exclaimed Noramary, flushing. Even as she spoke, she realized how the scene he had come upon could easily be misread and that her words had only served to confirm his suspicions.

"Obviously not," Duncan replied icily. "I've come to take you home." Turning to Robert, he made a stiff little bow. "My apologies, Mr. Stedd, if I have interrupted another reunion of old friends." He paused to let the reference to New Year's Eve take effect. Then, addressing himself directly to Noramary, he said, "My arrival is untimely, I see. It was not planned, but prompted by a surprise visit at Montclair. In the press of all the events of the winter, I'm afraid we failed to remember the portrait we commissioned Cecil Brandon to paint when he was at the Camerons' last fall. He is at Montclair at this moment, waiting to begin. So we must leave for home at once. The Camerons have graciously consented to entertain him until our return. This will explain why I had no opportunity to warn you of my coming."

Noramary tried to ignore the emphasis he put on the word *warn*.

"Of course. I will get ready right away," she murmured.

Over Aunt Betsy's protests, they left for Montclair the next day—Noramary, comfortably cushioned with afghans and pillows in the carriage, Duncan riding his horse alongside. Noramary was grateful for that. At least they would not have to endure the long ride in the chill atmosphere of Duncan's displeasure and suspicion.

The countryside she had left still locked in the bleakness of winter, had erupted into glorious springtime color, Noramary discovered upon her return, the woods around Montclair, a fairyland of pink and white dogwood blossoms. Even so, the old familiar feeling of dread swept over her as the carriage rolled into the drive. She felt almost like an escaped prisoner who had been captured and returned to gaol.

After a night's rest, Noramary sent word to Cecil Brandon at Cameron Hall that she would be ready to sit for him the following day.

Ellen had laid out the crimson velvet gown for the sitting. Now, as she helped Noramary with the buttons, she clucked in dismay. "Oh my, madam! This will have to be pinned to fit properly—you've wasted so! We must get some flesh on your bones. Some hearty Scotch porridge should do it!" she declared emphatically.

Brandon had dispatched a note to Noramary with directions for her to wear her hair very simply, adding with his flourishing hand: "Anything else would be gilding the lily." She put the finishing touches to the classic style he had requested, put in the ruby earrings and clasped the pendant on its chain around her neck. Without preamble, Duncan had simply sent in the case containing the Bridal Set.

Delva came in just then to announce that Mr. Brandon had come and was setting up his easel in the drawing-room corner that he had chosen because of its light.

Ellen beamed at her mistress. "Oh, madam, you look truly lovely. A picture, indeed!"

"Thank you, Ellen," Noramary said, smiling at her loyal housekeeper. "I don't fancy this whole thing much, I confess, but if it gives Duncan pleasure . . ."

"But, madam, you are the first bride to live in this house. He wants your portrait to hang in the front hall, like in the grand manor houses of England and Scotland. Then . . ." She paused and her eyes twinkled merrily, "the portraits of the brides your sons bring home will be hung next to yours."

For a moment the old pain seized Noramary's heart. But of course Ellen did not know that there would never be any Montrose sons! Why Duncan should insist on this portrait Noramary couldn't fathom.

Cecil Brandon surveyed his subject through narrowed eyes. Then seated her in a high-backed chair where the light streamed in through the windows. He took great pains arranging the folds of her gown, her hands with her unfurled fan just so. He tilted her head, moving it a fraction of an inch to the left, then, stepping back, moved it a little to the right. At last he stepped over to his easel, picked up his brush and palette, and announced, "Now we are ready to begin. I only hope I can do justice to your great beauty, my dear lady."

For what seemed a very long while to Noramary, there was no other sound in the room but that of the brush moving rapidly on the canvas as Brandon began blocking in her portrait. It was hard to sit so still. Her chin began to quiver from holding it at the angle in which he had positioned it. Her back began to ache and her fingers, holding the fan, to tingle. It seemed an eternity before Brandon put down his brush and said, "We'll take a short break now."

"May I see?" she asked, standing and arching her back to ease the stiff muscles.

"No, I never let my subjects see a portrait in the working stages—a rule I adhere to very strictly, in spite of the wiles of many beautiful ladies," he chuckled lightly. "And you, my dear, are among the most beautiful it has been my pleasure to paint."

Noramary blushed. She could never really think of herself as beautiful, despite this noted artist's word for it. Beautiful women had life handed to them on a silver platter, did they not? All the beautiful married women she knew, at least, had the love of their husbands—Jacqueline, Leatrice. . . .

Cecil Brandon was a man of cosmopolitan tastes, one who had traveled extensively and was as knowledgeable of many other topics as he was of painting. He was also a man of considerable sophistication, yet he was not in the least condescending. Noramary, had, at first, been awed by him, knowing his prestige as a painter of the great as well as of the nobility of England. But, as the sittings progressed, she lost her timidity in his presence and began to ask questions about his profession.

"Painting portraits is a very specialized branch of art," he told her. "One cannot improvise as an artist can in painting a landscape or still life; that is, put in a light or shadow or even add a piece of fruit or a flower if it will enhance the composition. A portrait painter must be true to what he sees. . . . Oh, I admit to having eliminated a wart or a wrinkle at times." He chuckled. "But in painting such perfection as yours, I'm hard put not to make the viewer think the artist has idealized his subject!"

Again Noramary felt uncomfortable. The compliment seemed too lavish for her own estimation of her looks.

She started to protest, when Cecil fixed her with a studied, penetrating look. "I have a feeling you don't like being beautiful. Perhaps it has caused you unhappiness?"

Noramary stared at him. It was almost as if she heard Nanny Oates speaking again. How could he know?

"Perhaps you find your beauty too heavy a burden? Perhaps it makes your husband jealous?"

Noramary looked at him incredulously. How had he discerned this?

As if reading her thoughts, he continued, "Ah, I suspected there was some cause for the decided change I find in you after only a few months' time. When I was here in the fall, you were radiant . . . all the glowing happiness of a bride newly wedded to a man she loves, who adores her! I find so great an alteration in you, there must be a deep, abiding problem. . . ."

Noramary was suddenly quiet, too quiet.

All at once it was too much to bear. Duncan's continued coldness, his distrust, his suspicion. It was too heavy a burden to carry alone any longer. Her eyes filled with tears. Speechless, she stared at Brandon. Sobs aching for release caused her to put two delicate hands to her throat, as if she were choking. Tears rolled unchecked down her cheeks.

The artist's perception somehow released all Noramary's pent-up emotions. Little by little, haltingly, Noramary poured out her story.

"I have come to believe that Duncan was still in love with Winnie when he married me. I don't think he realized that fully until. . . ." Here Noramary broke down again. "In the meantime, I had fallen deeply in love with him." She paused, then said in a voice that betrayed her bewilderment, "He thinks there is someone else in my life. A childhood friend, a very dear person whom I hold in great affection. But since the day I accepted Duncan, I have not tried to communicate with him nor to see him, except by chance. Somehow, no matter what I've said, my husband believes me to have been unfaithful!" she burst out. "I swear to you I have never been! He will not believe me, although I have told him over and over. I married him under circumstances that might have led him to think I did not love him. Perhaps I did not. I did not know what real love was then, though I took vows that were, and are, sacred to me. Perhaps, for a time, those vows were all that bound me to him—a promise made, a covenant to be kept. That, too, has changed. I have learned to love Duncan Montrose with a deep, abiding love, for I have seen him in moments of tenderness and gentleness. It is *that* Duncan I will go on loving, whether or not he ever believes that love . . . or accepts it."

Noramary put her head in her hands and wept brokenly.

"My dear lady, I have made you weep! Forgive me,

I should have said nothing . . . but there was such a marked difference, not only in your demeanor but in your whole expression . . . the eyes, the very mirror of the soul, are so sad. They reflect the pain in the heart. . . . I have not painted portraits for so many years for nothing. I could not help but observe . . ." Brandon said in some distress.

When her hard sobs finally lessened, Brandon lent her his clean linen handkerchief to wipe her eyes, and pressed her hand gently.

"Dear lady, sometimes one needs only a sympathetic ear to release healing tears. Perhaps our conversation has been fortuitous. I believe tomorrow the sitting will go better. Your candor and innocence will show forth. I will paint you so no one can question the shining beauty of your virtue." He smiled and gently touched the ruby earrings swinging from her ears, and quoted softly: "And who shall find a valiant wife, for her price is above rubies?"

"Even your stern husband will not be able to deny the fulfillment of the Bible's definition of a 'fortunate man.' He will read in your face the truth he has not been able to receive from your lips. Trust me, dear lady. Your portrait will be the finest work of my career."

Brandon quickly packed up his painting case and bid Noramary good-afternoon. He had been invited to the Camerons' for dinner, and Jacqueline had sent her carriage for him, which was even now waiting. He kissed Noramary's hand and left her sitting alone in the drawing room.

The afternoon sun was slanting through the long windows, and Noramary sat bathed in its rays, thinking over her confession and the artist's assurances. If it could only happen . . . if Duncan could only be convinced . . . if he could love her again. . . .

There was a noise behind her and instinctively she turned to see Duncan's tall figure standing in the archway, his height and broad shoulders filling it.

Her eyes, so recently misted with tears, were glistening, her lips parted in surprise, all color drained from her cheeks.

Noramary stood up, hands pressed against her breast where her heartbeat had quickened noticeably. She started to speak, but something restrained her. Several swift changes of expression passed over Duncan's face. He seemed to be struggling for words. So she waited. When he finally began to speak, his voice shook with emotion.

"Noramary, please understand that I did not mean to eavesdrop. I came into the house earlier than usual, intending to look in on the sitting, to see what progress Brandon had made on your portrait today. Perhaps it was intended that I should overhear your conversation." He stopped, flinging out both hands in a helpless gesture. "Maybe I should have left after hearing part of it—but I couldn't. I didn't.

"How can I explain? It all began the night we truly became man and wife. It was so glorious. I couldn't believe my good fortune—that the Lord had given me so precious a wife. Then, in your sleep, you whispered a name . . . a name that was not mine. And I foolishly jumped to conclusions." His tanned face flushed deeply. "I believed you and Robert Stedd . . . were more than friends.

"I was mad with jealousy. It seemed that after I'd found what I'd been waiting for for so long, it was no longer mine. I hardened my heart against you, so that everything else that happened met that barrier I'd erected between us. I was ready to think the worst." He halted, shaking his head as if it was almost too much for him to continue. "I didn't dare let you know how much you'd hurt me or how much what I *imagined* had hurt me. It made me too vulnerable. It was easier to build a stone wall around myself." He paused again. "But I couldn't stop loving you. If I couldn't have you as my true wife, I could at least carry an idealized image of you. . . ."

"The silhouette?" Noramary whispered.

Duncan looked surprised.

"I saw it," she explained.

"Yes, the silhouette . . . I persuaded Jacqueline to give it to me . . . but when . . ."

"I went out to the cottage that day I got lost in the woods, the day I became ill—"

"That terrible day I thought I'd lost you forever." Duncan sighed, a look of infinite pain on his face. "While you were lying ill, delirious, I stayed beside you, telling you how much I loved you, but of course, you could not hear. Then, in your room, I saw the letters on your desk, the one you had started to write to Robert, and all my dreams for our life together when you recovered were dashed. I thought they were love letters, that you and he had been corresponding behind my back all this time. Then when I came to Williamsburg and found you with him . . ." Duncan broke off. He hesitated, searching for the words to continue. "Noramary, what can I say? I was wrong. Terribly wrong. About you . . . about everything!"

For a long moment they stood without speaking, gazing at each other—one with eyes begging to be believed; the other, hoping she could trust what had been said.

Then Duncan held out his arms. After a pause he said, "Noramary, my love, forgive me . . . I've been so blind."

There was only a moment's hesitation before she went into those open arms with a sigh, and she felt the strength of his embrace enclose her.

All the sad uncertainty of the past months vanished. All her anxiety lifted. Something deeper than happiness began to grow, filling her with an incandescent gladness.

It was a moment Noramary never dreamed she would know. Before it, every other emotion dimmed to a mere shadow. It was everything known of poetry and music and passion . . . of joy and love and ecstasy. It had no beginning and no end.

At last she belonged, truly belonged. At last she could love and be loved . . . wholly . . . without fear or apology . . . completely . . . until the end of all time.

EPILOGUE

NORAMARY STIRRED, aware of some new sound penetrating the deep, dreamless sleep into which she had slipped, exhausted. The room was shadowy, with only the tawny glow from the fireplace giving some light. From her bed she could see out the window that against the gray blue February sky snow was gently falling. Leisurely snowflakes drifted, increasing in rapidity as she watched. It seemed that she and the world were wrapped in a velvety quiet.

As if from a long distance, she heard voices in the hall outside her door. It opened gently, letting in a shaft of light. Noramary turned her head slowly to see Ellen approaching the bed with a bundle in a lacy white shawl in her arms.

She came closer, bent nearer, laid the bundle in the curve of Noramary's arm. She felt its light weight against her heart. Her arms felt heavy, almost too tired to lift, and yet as the bundle stirred, a kind of excited wonder rose inside her. The baby! The last terrible hours were only faintly recalled as her hand cupped the tiny head and ran a finger over the downy tufts of hair. She felt something expand within her heart: love, happiness, a sort of rapture. Here was her baby.

"A handsome little boy, ma'am," Ellen announced proudly; as if she had produced him herself.

"A boy." Noramary murmured, peering into the little face. "A son for Duncan."

The child was so beautiful, his white skin transparently fine, the pearly shadows of his eyelids, the long lashes, the small, rosy cheeks, the tiny mouth with its short upper lip, the softness of the light brown hair, like a cap on the small, round head.

Afterward she slept for a long time. The next thing she knew, a tall figure was entering the bedroom, now shuttered against the evening, glowing with firelight. Moving lightly, quietly, for such a big man, Duncan came to the side of her bed, then knelt on the mounting steps and cradled her cheeks with his palms.

"My dearest love . . ." she heard him say, and a deep thrill trembled through her at the sound of his low voice.

"Duncan!" she whispered. "Are you pleased . . . a son?"

"*Our* son . . . Noramary. My darling." His voice faltered, nearly broke; his hand groped on the coverlet for her small one, grasped it. "I have never loved you more. You are more precious to me than I can ever say . . . I was afraid . . . I might lose you."

Noramary reached up and, touched his mouth with her fingers.

"There is no need for words, Duncan. I know now that you love me. Now we have—everything."

He kissed her fingertips and the palm of her hand as he turned it.

"Noramary, you will always be first . . . always." His voice was very slow, soft.

She must have drifted off again with Duncan holding her hand, because later, when she awakened, she was alone. From the little room above, Noramary could hear a low, crooning song. She smiled. Delva must have finally managed to get the baby away from Ellen and was rocking him in the nursery in the new cradle.

Weak but happy, Noramary floated back and forth from the euphoric half wakefulness to a sort of dreamlike state in which she felt all-knowing, all-powerful and prophetic.

She was so pleased that their first child was a boy, a son for Duncan, someone to carry on the name, the proud heritage of the Montrose clan with its long lineage going back into Scottish history.

She remembered what she and Duncan had talked about earlier.

"If you agree, darling, I should like to call the baby Cameron. They have been such good friends."

Cameron, she repeated to herself. Yes, she liked the name. It sounded strong and honorable, a fine name for their son and the heir to Montclair.

As difficult as it might be to imagine now, one day that small baby would be a man, and Montclair would be his. And one day he would bring his bride here, and they would have children—sons, who would then bring their brides here to this beautiful house that Duncan had built, which they were making into a home at last.

Perhaps, Noramary thought dreamily, there would be daughters, too, to be betrothed under the spreading branches of the newly planted elms or married in the lovely garden.

Noramary smiled to herself as she closed her eyes. Montclair would become legendary, like the love she and Duncan shared, triumphing over hardships, heartache, trials. Montclair, like their love, would survive through all the years to come.

She twisted the heavy gold and amethyst ring on her finger, the traditional ring given the Montrose brides thinking of the other women who would wear it.

She, Noramary Marsh, had been the first bride to come here . . . but not the last . . . no, not the last . . . she sighed happily.

ABOUT THE AUTHOR

JANE PEART is an author whose keen love of research and the Southland about which she writes are melded into one harmonious whole in this, the first novel of a brilliant series, THE BRIDES OF MONT-CLAIR.

Though the characters in future books will change, there is one constant—the magnificent house built on an original King's Grant in 1732. By the time the saga of the Montrose family begins, it is a generation removed from the dread sounds of war drums echoing through the vast forests around Montclair. It is a time when the influence of English manners, mores and culture is being felt and the American planter class is evolving.

A prolific writer, Jane is featured in the text, WRITING ROMANCE FICTION FOR LOVE AND MONEY, by Helen Schellenberg Barnhart. In addition, she is a frequent speaker at writers conferences throughout the country.

Jane currently resides with her husband in Eureka, California. They are the parents of two grown daughters who share their enthusiasm for the arts.

A Letter To Our Readers

Dear Reader:

Pioneering is an exhilarating experience, filled with opportunities for exploring new frontiers. The Zondervan Corporation is proud to be the first major publisher to launch a series of inspirational romances designed to inspire and uplift as well as to provide wholesome entertainment. In order that we might better contribute to your reading enjoyment, we would appreciate your taking a few minutes to respond to the following questions and return your response to:

> Anne Severance, Editor
> The Zondervan Publishing House
> 1415 Lake Drive, S.E.
> Grand Rapids, Michigan   49506

1. Did you enjoy reading VALIANT BRIDE?

   ☐ Very much. I would like to see more books by this author!
   ☐ Moderately
   ☐ I would have enjoyed it more if _____

2. Where did you purchase this book? _____

3. What influenced your decision to purchase this book?

   ☐ Cover   ☐ Back cover copy
   ☐ Title   ☐ Friends
   ☐ Publicity   ☐ Other _____

4. Please rate the following elements from 1 (poor) to 10 (superior).

- ☐ Heroine   ☐ Plot
- ☐ Hero   ☐ Inspirational theme
- ☐ Setting   ☐ Secondary characters

5. Which settings would you like to see in future Serenade/Serenata Books?

_____ _____

_____ _____

6. What are some inspirational themes you would like to see treated in future books?

_____ _____

_____ _____

7. Would you be interested in reading other Serenade/Serenata or Serenade/Saga Books?

- ☐ Very interested
- ☐ Moderately interested
- ☐ Not interested

8. Please indicate your age range:

- ☐ Under 18   ☐ 25–34   ☐ 46–55
- ☐ 18–24   ☐ 35–45   ☐ Over 55

9. Would you be interested in a Serenade book club? If so, please give us your name and address:

Name _____

Occupation _____

Address _____

City _____ State _____ Zip _____

Serenade Serenata Books are inspirational romances in contemporary settings, designed to bring you a joyful, heart-lifting reading experience.

Serenade Serenata books available in your local bookstore:

#1 ON WINGS OF LOVE, Elaine L. Schulte
#2 LOVE'S SWEET PROMISE,
   Susan C. Feldhake
#3 FOR LOVE ALONE, Susan C. Feldhake
#4 LOVE'S LATE SPRING, Lydia Heermann
#5 IN COMES LOVE, Mab Graff Hoover
#6 FOUNTAIN OF LOVE, Velma S. Daniels and
   Peggy E. King.
#7 MORNING SONG, Linda Herring
#8 A MOUNTAIN TO STAND STRONG,
   Peggy Darty
#9 LOVE'S PERFECT IMAGE, Judy Baer
#10 SMOKY MOUNTAIN SUNRISE,
   Yvonne Lehman
#11 GREENGOLD AUTUMN,
   Donna Fletcher Crow
#12 IRRESISTIBLE LOVE, Elaine Anne McAvoy
#13 ETERNAL FLAME, Lurlene McDaniel
#14 WINDSONG, Linda Herring
#15 FOREVER EDEN, Barbara Bennett
#16 THE DESIRES OF YOUR HEART,
   Donna Fletcher Crow
#17 CALL OF THE DOVE, Madge Harrah
#18 TENDER ADVERSARY, Judy Baer
#19 HALFWAY TO HEAVEN, Nancy Johanson
   Watch for other books in both the *Serenade Serenata* (contemporary) series coming soon:

#21 THE DISGUISE OF LOVE, Mary LaPietra
#22 THROUGH A GLASS DARKLY, Sara Mitchell

Serenade Saga Books are inspirational romances in historical settings, designed to bring you a joyful, heart-lifting reading experience.

Serenade Saga books available in your local bookstore:

#1   SUMMER SNOW, Sandy Dengler
#2   CALL HER BLESSED, Jeanette Gilge
#3   INA, Karen Baker Kletzing
#4   JULIANA OF CLOVER HILL,
      Brenda Knight Graham
#5   SONG OF THE NEREIDS, Sandy Dengler
#6   ANNA'S ROCKING CHAIR,
      Elaine Watson
#7   IN LOVE'S OWN TIME,
      Susan C. Feldhake
#8   YANKEE BRIDE, Jane Peart
#9   LIGHT OF MY HEART, Kathleen Karr
#10 LOVE BEYOND SURRENDER,
      Susan C. Feldhake
#11 ALL THE DAYS AFTER SUNDAY,
      Jeanette Gilge
#12 WINTERSPRING, Sandy Dengler
#13 HAND ME DOWN THE DAWN,
      Mary Harwell Sayler
#14 REBEL BRIDE, Jane Peart
#15 SPEAK SOFTLY, LOVE, Kathleen Yapp
#16 FROM THIS DAY FORWARD, Kathleen Karr
#17 THE RIVER BETWEEN, Jacquelyn Cook

Watch for other books in the *Serenade Saga* series coming soon:

#19 WAIT FOR THE SUN, Maryn Langer
#19 HOLD FAST THE DREAM,
      Lurlene McDaniel
#21 LOVE'S GENTLE JOURNEY, Kay Cornelius
#22 APPLEGATE LANDING, Jean Conrad